SISTER'S DIRTY SECRET

Meg Oliphant

Sister's Dirty Secret

Past Venus Press
London 2007

Past Venus Press

is an imprint of

THE *Erotic* Print Society

EPS, 1st Floor, 17 Harwood Road,
LONDON SW6 4QP

Tel: +44 (0) 207 736 5800
Email: eros@eroticprints.org
Web: www.eroticprints.org

© 2007 MacHo Ltd, London UK

ISBN : 978-1-904989-33-2

Printed and bound in Spain by S.A de Litografia. Barcelona

SISTER'S DIRTY SECRET

Meg Oliphant

EPS

VIETNAM

The two men jogged down the street laughing, looking up in wonder at the vast, slate-grey clouds, pregnant with rain, that now contrasted so dramatically with the sunlit dazzle of low whitewashed buildings on either side.

"It's here. I'm fucking sure it's round here somewhere. Madame Soo's or Fu's or something."

Don looked at the big Australian and began laughing again.

"Shit, Greg, you Aussies couldn't find your cock in your pants, man. Admit it, you're completely lost."

It was late afternoon and the two friends were both a little drunk and horny as hell. They stopped an old man wearing a pale blue cotton tunic and *non*, the conical peasant straw hat, and asked him.

"Hey, old man, you heard of Madame Fu round these parts?"

The old man grinned and took a step closer, looking up at them from under the brim of his hat.

"Ah, you mean Mama Nu! Oh yes, you boys like. You get good yumyum there. Very good."

He cackled and made an obscene, jerky movement with his hand and opened his almost toothless mouth to mime the act of oral sex.

"You give me 100 piastres – I show you."

They gave him the money without

haggling. They'd had enough of wandering around the district and they wanted another drink and the girls. And then it started to rain. The old man led the way, seemingly indifferent to the roar of the downpour hitting the tin roofs or the warm rain that pelted them so hard it almost hurt, and soon had them drenched. He banged on a door and a little window opened up. A lively exchange took place. The door was unlocked and they went in, leaving the old boy to scuttle off into the downpour.

It's a nice place, thought Don. Clean. Good, modern furniture. In some ways it wasn't unlike the much larger, officially sanctioned, Pleiku brothel that he'd visited with the big Australian pilot a few days back.

Don knew that the main reason the U.S. Army provided establishments like the Pleiku was the same for any field brothel – to look after the soldiers' welfare. There was the chance that one of the whores could be a Viet Cong agent out to pick up useful information from her trusting bedmates. So the girls were not just carefully selected on the basis of how nice and cute they were and how well they spoke English. As well as getting a medical, the U.S. Army Intelligence would carefully screen each girl. The girls were closely supervised by some sort of *Mamasan* employed by the Pleiku Administrative Council. An American

GI paid 300 piastres – about $2.50 – for a ticket, allowing him up to three hours with any given prostitute. As if on a conveyor belt, up to 300 grunts visited the house each day, passing through a sandbagged guard post where they were required to show their ticket and have it stamped by a Vietnamese soldier. The centre then deducted 15% of the girl's earnings to pay for its expenses, but a hard-working and popular prostitute could still earn between 8,000 to 15,000 piastres ($66 to $125) a month, which was a damned good salary in wartime Vietnam. Considering a South Vietnamese government minister had a fixed salary of only $120 a month. Despite the welcome sense of security all this provided, as Don and his Aussie friend Greg soon discovered, there was a depressing conformity about the place: twosomes, threesomes, foursomes and moresomes were not allowed and overstaying your three-hour welcome was also off the menu.

So not surprisingly, most of the soldiers preferred to look for prostitutes themselves in bars that catered to GIs. They were more fun. The girls did a lot of interesting things with their pussies. Like smoke Marlboros with them, shoot out a dart or a ping-pong ball or open a bottle of beer. The agenda would always go something like this: the first night of R&R, get loaded, get laid, get loaded, get laid, get loaded and shack up for the night with your favourite bar girl.

But this sort of fun and games with bar girls meant taking risks: 'Vietnam Rose' – a strain of gonorrhoea so-called because the knob-end of your dick swelled up like a big pink rose – had reached almost epidemic proportions among GI's and slowly the message got through that there was nothing sissy about wearing a rubber. Outrageous rumours circulated about an incurable strain of syphilis, called 'Black Clap' or Viet Cong girls who were able to put razor blades into their vaginas to castrate or even kill clients. These deterred some from consorting with bar girls altogether, but not many. The lure of that sweet Asian pussy was simply too strong.

And it was in one of these bars that Don and Greg had suddenly decided to try out the new place. They'd spent the morning running through the catalogue of problems and potential woes that faced the intrepid brothel hound. Greg had suggested they look for a place recommended by one of the South Vietnamese officers he'd met. 'Safe' girls. Nice, clean place. Not too expensive.

It sounded like a dream.

And, on the whole, it lived up to its reputation. Better still; they could take on three or more girls at once, a new experience for Don, but one that his new friend Greg swore by with an enthusiasm that was positively infectious.

"Strewth, Don, you just haven't lived until you've partied with more than one poontang at a time. It's crazy!" And Don had to admit that he was in no position to contradict him, his multiple 'poontang' experience being what it was – not exactly impressive.

In the end, Mama Nu's had only boasted five girls. Don and Greg had sat in comfortable armchairs; the girls had paraded naked in front of them while the men sipped their bourbon and ice highballs. It was weirdly reminiscent of a police line up where you had to identify a suspect, thought Don. But then the girls were all pretty: full sensuous mouths, high cheekbones, and innocent young faces. Expressive almond eyes – half playful, smiling, yet strangely wistful. Graceful, feminine bodies swayed and danced in front of the two men, causing them to almost drool with excitement. Some girls were slim, with pert, tip-tilted breasts so perfect in shape and size that they almost made Don gasp with pleasure; and just looking at those rounded, sassy little derrières made his cock lurch in his pants. Others were more curvaceous and more mature-looking but no less beguiling. Luscious, dark brown nipples set on golden skin; small, yet womanly, bodies with hourglass contours. Pussies that were either surprisingly well covered with black pubic hair or almost devoid of it. Don looked over at Greg and saw the big Aussie's shorts tenting. He looked down at his own groin and realised that his own hard-on was almost painfully attempting to escape the confines of his lightweight cotton pants.

Each of the girls wore a little beaded bracelet from which hung a numbered disc so they could be identified easily. Mama Nu herself was a fat, permanently smiling, bustling lady in a colourful silk *áo dài* who could have been anywhere between the ages of thirty-five and forty-five. She told the men to remember the numbers of the girls they liked and then she shooed her young charges out of the room amid little shrieks and much giggling.

"You boys take two girls each? Three girls? You have special price for two girls! Not expensive!"

Business, it seemed, was slack. This time, the men haggled, but without much conviction. Outside it was still raining stair-rods, the price was fair and Madame Fu could see their hard-ons, so she knew she held all the cards.

"Tell you what, Greg, you take your best three and I'll be cool with a deuce."

"You sure about that, mate?"

"Absolutely. Remember, I'm a beginner at

this numbers game."

And so it was decided. Greg grinned. Mama Nu beamed as she counted the money. Don ended up with two of the beautiful, smiling young prostitutes and three giggling girls disappeared into a separate room with Greg. It seemed everyone was happy.

Everyone except Don.

Despite his horniness, he suddenly thought of Kathy back home in Santa Monica. Shit! What a time to get some sort of stupid guilt-complex about her. Why, she's probably so frustrated she's screwing old man Fuldman, their neighbour, right now. The thought of this coupling was so absurd that he cracked an involuntary smile. Then a grin, then he took another swig of whisky, tipped his head back and roared with laughter.

Diu was the sweet, tender one, new and not yet experienced. Xuan was the older of the two, a cheeky little trollop who knew every trick in the book. First they stripped him naked. Then they sponged him down with warm soap and water and dried him with small hand towels. It was a miracle that he didn't shoot his load there and then. He lay on the bed, face down. Gradually he became accustomed to their delicate little hands wandering over his body, poking, prying, kneeding and stroking. Then he turned over. There was a sharp intake of breath from Diu and an earthy laugh from Xuan.

"You very big!" said Diu in awed tones as her colleague rolled a rubber onto him.

"You got nice cock!" said Xuan, swinging her thigh over him and grabbing his erect penis to thrust into her pussy that had become wet enough to accommodate his entire length without any real difficulty.

Don was relieved. If she'd taken his cock in her sexy, full-lipped mouth just then, he would have shot his load without any doubt. This way – with the girl on top – was better.

She started to rise and fall on his hard cock, her face a mixture of mirth and lust. Don was in heaven. Despite the thin rubber membrane, the sensations produced by her young oriental vagina were out of this world. She said something to Diu. The willowy young girl positioned herself with awkward, coltish movements so that she faced Xuan. Don looked up into the golden, twin mounds of the most delectable ass he had ever seen. He brought his hands up to separate the perfect globes, admiring the soft, almost hairless pussy lips and further up, the dark brown pucker of young Diu's little asshole. He lifted his head and swiped his tongue along her cleft, eliciting a little moan from above. Although the outer pussy lips were dry, he soon detected a slippery juiciness within that betrayed the younger prostitute's excitement. She rocked her hips back and forth to get more enjoyment from Don's tongue, now busily licking and sucking her soft, blood-swollen labia.

Turning his head, he could see the girls' reflection in the big framed looking glass that had been hung on the wall by the bed, presumably for just this sort of view. They were kissing and stroking each other's breasts, sucking and tweaking the nipples. This show was not for his benefit. There was no pretence here, just girlish passion and enjoyment of their lovely, sensuous young bodies. It was too much for the virile young pilot.

"Oh fuck...," sighed Don as he spurted uncontrollably into the prophylactic.

Later they had all dozed off together in the big bed. When Don woke up, Diu had gone to get more drinks and Xuan had produced a joint. After an hour or so, Don was hard again. This time he fucked little Diu, doggy-style, while Xuan got behind him to tongue his anus and lick the back of his ballsack. The sensation had been amazing. He held on to Diu's slim hips, reached below to grope her perky little tits and pinch her hard nipples; somehow he had managed to exert enough self-control to stop himself from shooting into her extremely tight little quim. When he was nearly ready to come, when he knew he couldn't hold off for much longer, he made Xuan rest her head in the small of Diu's back. Xuan's eyes narrowed with lust as she watched his cock repeatedly plough into the narrow pink cleft of Diu's tight cunt. Finally he pulled out and, tearing off the rubber, squirted his creamy load between the older girl's thick, open lips. She suckled him gently and squeezed his balls as if to milk the last drops of jissum into her mouth. A thin white trickle coasted down over her chin. Xuan held his gaze as she swallowed noisily, then grinned and opened her mouth wide. "See? All gone now. Me swallow all your cock-juice!" And both girls laughed and kissed each other, pink tongues cleaning away any traces of Don's cum.

The next day they were back at base, a little hung-over, it was true, but relaxed and ready to rock and roll with the Vietcong.

Chapter 1

It was a lovely morning. But, then, it was always a lovely morning in Santa Monica. Mr. Fuldman, retired, henpecked, was out tending his garden bright and early. His wife was pleased with his sudden interest in gardening. Actually, old Fuldman didn't care a hang about flowers or lawns, they were all weeds to him. What he did care about and why he was out in the garden bright and early every morning was for the pleasure and excitement of seeing their neighbor, young Kathy Walters, walk out of her house and down to the mailbox and then back up the path again.

On what Fuldman called "good days" she would open the mail then walk slowly back up the path to the house. The slower, the better, for Fuldman's interests. This particular morning, he positioned himself in a corner of the yard, crouching over a bed of marigolds and pretending to dig while his eyes looked through his bushy eyebrows and he waited.

And Kathy was well worth the waiting.

Yesterday, she had come down to the mailbox dressed in a lounging gown and old Fuldman had gritted his teeth against his anger at being disappointed then almost fell in a bed of tulips as, while she was opening the mail, her gown fell open and he saw one leg up to the hip bone. It was an indelible image he would savor late at night while lying next to his snoring wife. She was wearing high heels under the gown and her leg showed itself off beautifully with slim tapered ankles curving out into well-rounded calves. Then – and every time Fuldman thought of it, his mouth went dry – a thigh. Not just any thigh, but full, voluptuous thighs that seemed to swoop out in pure white firmness. And all she was wearing was a rose-red bikini panty!

Fuldman had to close his eyes when he thought of how the panties stretched tight across her hips, revealing the soft bulge of one pelvic bone and the way the material caught tight and was tense at the V of her crotch.

It was only for a split second, but old Fuldman had seen it and found himself shaking. "By God, if I were only twenty years younger!" he had muttered.

The postman had delivered the mail, turned the flag up and Fuldman was in position. His only regret was the fact that he couldn't get closer.

Kathy Walters came out of the house.

She had risen early, determined to clean. It was such a bright and sunny day, she saw no reason for wearing a lot of clothes. A pair of shorts and one of Don's old white shirts pulled and knotted around her slim waist seemed enough. She came from the house barefoot and old Fuldman crouched like some old satyr and peered through his white picket fence.

Kathy came down the path tossing her hair. It was beautiful jet-black hair and contrasted sharply with her pale blue eyes. The tights were old and rose high on her hips, almost revealing her hip bones. A pair of hip huggers she had cut off, they slung low, revealing her navel which Fuldman saw with rippling flesh. The V of the huggers fit tight over her crotch. Kathy enjoyed the slight pressure and excitement they afforded her and walked in a hip undulating fashion to heighten the sensation.

Old Fuldman fell to one knee as he craned forward, his now sweating face no more than three inches from the fence as he saw her bending to open the mailbox. My God! he thought, that young chippie isn't wearing a bra!

It was true. Her ample breasts seemed to shift under her husband's shirt and the nipples made little reverse indentations on the cotton, sticking out in a provocative way.

Fuldman quickly swiped at his upper lip,

removing perspiration. Kathy was a lovely thing to look at: slim, big breasted, long legs, thick hair and a lovely face with a small nose, almost snub-nosed, and a large, sensuous mouth. She looked just like the girls he saw in Playboy magazine whenever he went down to the drugstore to get prescriptions filled. She was better than anything he had ever seen in a magazine. She was real! And she was across the street, tearing open a letter and practically naked.

As he watched, she read a letter hastily, a smile coming over her face. Then, in a spontaneous movement, she jumped up and down with glee, her breasts shaking and quivering.

To his disappointment, she turned to run to her house. Then, his luck holding, she dropped a letter and bent over, her back to him, and picked it up. For one moment of glorious agony, Fuldman saw her hips and buttocks fan out and her shorts ride high up and be caught in the deep crevice between her legs. She straightened and walked on to the house, the two smooth, undulating cheeks of her buttocks in plain sight bouncing up and down.

If it had been any other day and any other letter, Kathy might have heard a moan from the yard across the way and looked to see what was happening. But, not today. She held in her hand THE letter. Everybody gets at least one letter in their life which they can deem important. They can look back to that time and say, "My life changed that day."

So it was for Kathy. She ran into the house excited, not knowing what she was going to do or if there was anything she should do.

She stood in their living room and laughed softly. She read the letter again, taking in every word. It was so very brief.

DARLING, LEAVING THIS HELLHOLE IN ONE WEEK AND FLYING BACK HOME TO YOU. LOVE, DON.

Airmailed and postmarked two days ago. A quick calculation told her he might be home by next weekend. Kathy felt good, better than she had felt in weeks. If old Fuldman hadn't been so interested in her body and his own frustrated thoughts, he would have noticed that Kathy wasn't a happy girl; that she was, in fact, a deeply troubled human being. If horny old Fuldman had looked closely, he would have seen the telltale signs of much drinking the night before.

Don had been in Vietnam a year and she had lived alone, having few friends and occasionally working for the Kelly Girls, taking office jobs when they seemed suitable and the mood hit her. Most of her friends were the wives of servicemen, like herself, waiting for their men to come home.

Then Ned, her younger brother came to visit her and stay. Although a warm day, Kathy shivered, thinking about him and his visit. At home, when they were growing up, Ned, one year younger, had always been a wild one, getting into all sorts of trouble. At first, it had been dismissed as "coltish behavior", and "sowing his wild oats." Later, it had gotten more serious: drinking escapades and stories of wild parties. Ned ran with a crowd that was considered disreputable and Kathy had nothing to do with them. One night Ned had come home drunk and surprised Kathy as she lay in bed reading a book. He had attacked her. The word "attack" was never really mentioned and the whole thing was smoothed over as a joke. Ned being so drunk he "didn't know where he was." At least that is what Kathy's mother had said. Her mother had a special attachment to Ned that Kathy used to wonder about. Near forty, her mother was still a fine looking woman.

When Don came along, the whole world changed and it wasn't long before they were married and moved to Santa Monica. And then Kathy's mother wrote to say that Ned was coming out to see her right after school let out. Ned was attending an eastern college. In his first year, he had been almost kicked out. Several students had been arrested in an apartment off campus. Seems a sex party had been going on and one girl claimed that she had been raped.

And Ned had come to visit Kathy.

Despite his sardonic and unpredictable ways, Kathy loved her brother. His aggressiveness and his sharp tongue didn't bother her; she thought, that with time, he would change. When he first came, she had been struck by how different they were. She was to learn, to her horror and shame, how very much alike they were in at least one way.

He had showed up one morning in front of her house, a sleeping bag on his back, his hair too long and unkempt, his lips twisted in that old grin. "Hiya. Man, you're something else."

After she had fed him and he talked of their parents, she sat down across the table from him and looked at him carefully. He had grown, he was no longer just her little brother, he was a man. And that same mischievous look was on his face. Only, now, there was something more there. The impish quality had become hard, there was a glitter and gleam to his eye that disturbed her. What was it? It seemed to her they were shrewd eyes old beyond belief. There was a cynical edge to his voice, a strange dry quality that told you there was little that he hadn't done.

Standing with Don's scrawled hasty letter in her hand, Kathy shivered again. She slumped into a chair and stared off. What was she going to do? How could she tell Don? What would happen, how would she feel when Don was finally in front of her took her in his arms? How would she respond? Would it be the same as before?

Or, would she, in some unpredictable way, give herself away? How would she act in the throes of passion?

Her depression came back and she felt the need of a drink. Just one, she told herself, then put her hand to her head and closed her eyes. She had to face this thing, she had to think it out. More than anything, she had to resolve it in her own mind.

She had been always told and felt it was true that she was a person of character. Setting her jaw, she carefully folded Don's letter and put it away in the desk with all of his letters that she had kept. She could not resist sitting and rereading some of them, tears brimming in her eyes. She loved Don and he was the only man ever to have her... until Ned, her brother, came to visit.

She couldn't stand it any longer. She slammed the desk drawer shut then swiveled to the kitchen where she poured a drink of scotch into a glass and sat down at the kitchen table. I don't care if it's morning and this is a stupid thing to do. I want to think, she told herself.

She swallowed the scotch and made a face, feeling it burn down and hit her empty stomach. Hastily, she made some instant coffee and poured the rest of the scotch in the cup and sat down to sip and think.

One of the wonders of the human mind is its adaptability. Kathy had not once allowed herself to think of what happened with Ned since he had gone. While it was happening and while he was staying with her, she could think of nothing else. When he left, something in her brain shut off. An instinct told her she needed time to think, to recover. She became busy with hundreds of chores. She visited girl friends and baby sat. She went alone to movies and when she had seen them all, when there was nothing to do or no one to see, when it was night and she was alone with only the TV playing endlessly, she drank. She drank heavily and many mornings awoke to find herself still on the couch, clothed, with the television hissing a pale blue screen in the corner. Her head would ache and her stomach was sour and she took long showers and plenty of aspirin.

And she dreaded becoming a secret drinker, a furtive alcoholic.

She would sit for hours, smoking, drinking, longing for Don and wanting so much to talk with him. Then, thinking of what happened, she dreaded the idea of Don coming back to her; she was not the same person he had left.

She sipped steadily on her coffee and inhaled the fumes of the scotch and willed herself to think of what had happened and try to understand it and the way that she felt.

Ned, restless the first night, insisted they go out. He had money and wanted to see the town. They had gone out for drinks and dinner and Ned had grown funnier and more charming as the night went on. Driving in the car, Kathy had said, "Where to now?"

"Nirvana, Babe."

"Huh? "

"A little action." "Gee, I don't know. I don't go out much now that Don's away. I've been out of it. How about a movie?"

Ned slumped down in his seat and made a face. "How about a taffy pull or a night class in wax casting? Come on, Babe, you can do better than that."

Kathy smiled at her brother who looked so bored. "Okay, what do you want to do?"

"A nightclub. One of those topless-bottomless joints. A real sleazy dive with lots of broads around and guys trying to make time."

Kathy raised her eyebrows. "Somehow I don't think I'm the person to ask about that. Besides, you're only nineteen. You couldn't get in."

Ned pointed a finger at her and made a popping sound with his mouth. "I gotta phoney I.D."

"Isn't that against the law?

"Sure, if you're dumb enough to get caught. Look, who's going to say my I.D. is phoney? I left my real one back at your place. Where's a strip joint?"

"I don't know if I should go to such a place?"

"Ever seen one?"

"No."

"Then don't knock it if you don't know about it. Aren't you at all curious?"

Kathy smiled despite herself. It was almost as if he could read her thoughts. In fact, she was very curious in what really went on in what she and Don called "The topless pits." Since Don had been in Vietnam, she had abstained from sex, feeling a great yearning and loneliness yet feeling that it was all worth it. When her man came home, he would come to her bed and it all would be just beautiful. Now, Ned had tickled her curiosity and she felt this was a perfect time to satisfy it: she couldn't go with girl friends because it would look funny, like they were trying to "get picked up." She certainly couldn't go with another man and square it with her conscience. But she could go with Ned. He was not just another man, he was her brother. She could, when in a teasing mood, tell Don she had been in a topless bar and feel no guilt, because Ned had been along.

The delicious sense of doing something wrong, a child-like fit of giggles came over her. "I know where a lot of those places are."

"Take me there, you improper bitch!" Ned said, clowning and waving an arm.

They were in a gay mood full of nonsense when they entered a club, THE PUSSYCAT PARLOR. Kathy found herself, once inside, in pitch blackness. She blinked and held her hand out. Ned, thoroughly accustomed to such dark, led her along through the tables. There was a bright stage light at the far end of the dark bar and Kathy knew that would be where the "action" was. She didn't look at it; half out of excitement and half out of her footing as they weaved toward the light.

They were seated at a ringside table by a girl in a lowcut blouse showing plenty of cleavage. When Kathy sat down she saw that the girl was wearing black tights and panties that were cut so as to ride high up on her hip. The girl smiled invitingly at Ned and took their order. Music was blaring from a jukebox and Kathy caught a movement out of the corner of her eye. A girl, young, attractive, with long hair and an Indian headband across her forehead, mounted the stage. She was dressed in a simple miniskirt and she smiled down at them, her body already beginning to sway and move to the rock beat.

Very simply, with a smile that was relaxed and a little lewd, she pulled the dress up over her head and Kathy gasped. The girl was naked, save for her sandals and headband!

Kathy knew she had a good body, but this girl was really good. She was tall, willowy, with a long waist and full firm hips. Her long tapering thighs came down to dimpled knees and long calves ending in incredibly thin ankles. Her breasts were high and huge and jutting out, away from each other and ended in taut nipples like two dark bullets. Her stomach was flat and her buttocks, seen in the mirrors behind her were two full smooth cheeks with a deep crevice dividing them.

Kathy's astonished eyes took her all in and finally centered, hopelessly fascinated, by the V of soft curling pubic hair that formed where her deep thighs met her torso. Her mound of Venus jutted out ever so enticingly, only to serve notice as to the hidden delights of the warm inviting vagina hidden up between her thighs.

Hands on her hips, the girl gyrated in time to the building music, looking down at Ned and Kathy and slowly licking her lips as her hips rotated. As the music grew wilder, the girl began shaking her shoulders, making her breasts quiver in a lascivious way and her hands slid down to cup around her groin, to feel the air as if she were caressing an invisible penis and to jut her hips out in a lewd invitation. Kathy's mouth fell open as she looked up at the girl dancing and saw the swelling lips of her vagina beginning to ever-so-slightly part as she danced on.

My God, Kathy thought, she's getting herself really aroused!

She had never seen a woman do this before in private, let alone in public. The music became more frantic, louder, and the girl became more abandoned in her dancing, doing deep bends and leaning over and wiggling her buttocks invitingly, her breasts moving in a tantalizing way. It dawned on Kathy that the girl was actually dancing a sex act – the woman's half of the sex act – right in front of everyone. The music grew wilder. and the girl's hair lashed around as she threw her head back and spread her legs, a look of ecstasy on her face as her hips undulated and she spread her legs wider and Kathy could clearly see the narrow glistening slit of her naked cunt.

Everyone could see. Kathy's head was going around as she watched, not even conscious that their drinks had been served and that she was gulping at it. Her heart was pounding and every nerve in her body, so long quiet, was now hammering at her being. The natural thought came into her mind: what must it be like to do that?

And the answer, with a force and fury that amazed her, told her it would be exciting. The girl in front of them, totally naked, her eyes half closed, her mouth open and her lips wet, her body writhing, moving sensuously to the wild music, was obviously enjoying every minute of it.

The music stopped and the girl forced herself to stop too. She pulled her dress on, breathing hard, looking down at Ned with a strange searching look on her face. Kathy looked at him and saw that lopsided little enigmatic grin on his face. Still looking at him, the girl slipped off behind a partition.

"Wow, she was all right. You like that? You sure know how to pick the places, Babe," Ned said, flicking his fingers to order another round of drinks.

Kathy put one hand to her face, shielding it from the rest of the bar. "I've never seen anything like that before in my whole life. I never dreamed! She didn't have anything on!"

"That's right. Groovy. Nothing like getting down to the old nitty-gritty."

"Is that legal? I mean, supposing the police raid this place?"

Ned's expression of disgust came again.

"Sister, I gotta say this. You are square. Don't you know what's been happening? Where have you been since you left home? The law can't do a thing. Their hands are tied. It had something to do with the Supreme Court. They can't touch an operation like this. It's art, baby!"

They were served their drinks and Kathy gulped again. She was still astounded and excited. She felt the urge to squirm against the hot throbbing and moistness she felt down between her legs. The sheer brazen audacity of it all numbed her except for a strangely rising sexual response that she couldn't control.

And her younger brother, sitting across from her with that inscrutable sardonic smile, watching her with those cold attentive eyes. Ned, so wild and unpredictable, so young and so handsome. Ned, toying with his drink and grinning. "Let's go home."

Kathy caught her breath and looked around. "We just got here."

"I wanna go. I wanna talk to you."

The tone of his voice had sent a warning bell ringing in her mind. But the alcohol, the dancing girl, her own thwarted desire overrode the sound. He was after all, her brother. "Okay."

In the car again, they drove saying little, Kathy driving with Ned staring moodily out the passenger side window. Back in the apartment, Ned sprawled on the couch and looked up at his sister, that ironic smile coming back. "What do you like?"

Kathy was genuinely puzzled. "What do I like?"

"Yeah, what turns you on in bed? What kind of sex do you like?"

Kathy was visibly jarred by the question and she had skipped a beat before laughing and saying, with a wave of the hand, "Oh, lots of things. Want a drink?"

Ned got up. "No, I got something better." He went to the closet and got out his sleeping bag. Not looking at her, he asked, "Ever make it with more than one guy? Ever try a threesome?"

Kathy felt her body tingle. "What?"

Ned appeared a bit weary. "ever ball two guys at the same time?"

Kathy again visibly reacted as the image of Don, herself, and a faceless man whipped into her mind. It was so exciting and depraved, she couldn't allow herself to think about it. "I... I don't think that's any of your business," she said, turning to the bar Don had built before leaving and pouring herself a drink.

"Okay," Ned said, ambling back to the couch with some cigarette papers in his hand and a little pouch dangling from one finger.

"What's that?" Kathy asked, her voice

full of suspicion.

"Grass," Ned said casually.

Kathy set her drink down firmly on the bar. "No," she said in a firm tight voice. All of a sudden, she was feeling a dislike for her brother.

Ned grinned at her as he measured out the green dried weeds. "Come on. Mean to say you've never tried it?"

"No." Kathy stood in front of him. "Ned, I won't have that kind of stuff in my house."

"Huh?"

"I mean it and I'm ashamed of you, doing a thing like that. Shame on you."

Ned looked at her for a minute before bursting out in incredulous laughter. "You really mean it. You're not putting me on? You really mean it, this is no put-on?"

"Yes."

"Well that sure puts a tail on the dog. You've never tried this?"

"No, and I don't want to."

"Don has."

Again, his calmness, his laughing face, and his ability to change pace threw her. "How do you know?"

Again, Ned laughed. "Hell, he's in Vietnam."

Kathy's face clouded. It was true, there had been articles in the papers about pot smoking among the troops. "You're only guessing," she said defiantly.

He shook his head. "I know Don."

"That's no reason for me to try it," she said, walking back to her drink.

"There's every reason in the world for you to try it."

Again, Kathy was puzzled by her brother. "What do you mean by that?"

Now, looking back, Kathy could see that was the wrong question to ask. Had she insisted he get rid of the stuff, the ensuing argument might never have happened and the whole evening might have been different.

Ned had answered her question, had talked long about "grass" and had played on her doubts and fears, gradually boxing her in until Kathy, feeling she was insane, feeling that she was doing something sinful and depraved, agreed to take "just one puff". She did it, holding her breath as long as she could, then exhaled. "I don't feel a thing."

Ned had smiled secretly. "Wait," was all he would say.

Having taken one puff and felt nothing, it didn't seem so terribly dangerous to take another. And a third. Fourth. She took so many puffs, she lost track of how many drags she had. In fact, she seemed to have lost track of time itself. There was so much she suddenly couldn't account for. They were sitting on the floor with drinks in front of them and music was playing on the radio and had been playing for a long time. She was smoking a cigarette and watching, with a glazed absorption, the thick gray smoke curling up in the air. It seemed that she had been watching the smoke all night.

"I have."

Ned's quiet voice made her jump. She tried to focus on him. "What?" she asked, her voice thick and slurring.

"I've balled two chicks at the same time."

"What?" Kathy said stupidly, feeling a wave of lewd curiosity come over her.

"Yeah," Ned went on, smiling. "Two girls. Met them in a commune I visited and they liked that sort of thing."

"Really? That's terrible," Kathy said with a little giggle.

"What are you laughing for if it's terrible?"

"I don't know. I feel so... funny."

"Yeah." Leaning over, he began stroking the back of her arm. Despite herself, she let him do it. It felt so good, sending a tingling sensation all through her body.

"What did you do?" She couldn't help asking the question as she bit her lip in anticipation.

Ned kept on stroking her arm, running his fingers up to her shoulder. "I balled them. We fucked."

The word "Fucked," hung in the air and Kathy felt an involuntary tingle down between her legs as she heard the word. Her legs were crossed and she wondered hazily if he could see up her dress to her panties.

Looking down at her drink, she asked, "And... what did... they, the girls, do?"

"They took turns fucking me and then went down on each other while I watched." His other hand began stroking one of her knees, pushing her skirt back.

Kathy's heart was pounding and her mouth was dry. Her mind was imagining what it must have been like and paying no attention to what his hands were doing. Besides, it felt good, exciting her and making the idea of her own brother in bed with two women all the more exciting. It was wrong, it was evil, it was depraved, it was carnal, yet it was exciting. She had looked at her brother full of dazed, drugged wonder. He had actually done such a thing! It was unbelievable. "You're making all this up."

Thinking back, reliving every moment of the night with her brother, Kathy put her head in her hands and wanted to cry. If only she had gotten up at that point, or at least forced his hands away, it might have been different.

Yet, now, she knew it would have been

the same. Details might have changed, but the end result would be the same. Ned had wanted it to happen and, now, only now, could Kathy, full of despair, admit that she too had wanted it to happen.

Chapter 2

She had no chance. She was drugged, she had no idea of how much she had drunk. Ned was telling her lurid details about his night in bed with the two girls, describing their bodies and what they did to him in lewd detail, and his hands were all over her body.

Ned had said she was too tense. How had he put it?

"You're uptight. Relax." Thinking of his exact words, she went back to the night, determined to relive the whole thing. He had suggested a massage and she had stretched out on the floor on her stomach and felt his strong hands kneading the flesh around her neck and shoulders. "Oh, that feels so good! she had sighed.

And she let him go on. Her own younger brother had unzipped her dress and his fingers gently massaged her bare flesh. She had only murmured when he had unclasped her bra. She lay quiet, sighing with pleasure as his hands caressed her back and she felt an intense pleasure that somehow lulled her mind while pleasing her body. This was the first time she had felt any physical affection since Don had left and it was so pleasant and everything was happening so easily as Ned said, "I can't get at your arms and shoulders with this dress in the way."

And Kathy had actually helped him get it off until she was lying with the dress down around her waist, her whole back naked, her breasts crushed under her in the bra. It was wrong what she was doing, naughty, bad, but so very very good. And, after all, she rationalized through the marijuana haze, it was her brother.

The music, light and dreamy, was still playing on the radio and Kathy found herself listening in rapt pleasure as she felt his hands working their way down her spinal cord, toward her buttocks. Her excitement increased as she felt his fingers probing lower and lower, pulling down her panties until his fingers were working soothingly at the deep crevice between her buttocks. Just as she felt she must say something to stop him, he returned to her shoulders, gripping them as he leaned over and whispered, "That feel good, Sis?"

"Mmmmm," she had murmured and he began all over again. She closed her eyes as she felt the fingers on her back. They were strong and sure and she liked the feeling and a wild thought filtered through her drug dimmed mind... just once, one time in my life, I'd like to be in an orgy with other naked people. Just once!

His hands were going lower this time, slowly going over her back to tease themselves in the soft yielding crevice of her buttocks. His hand was actually under her white nylon panties now and just inches from her now unprotected anus that suddenly became alive with feeling and she was aware of her vagina, pressed into the rug underneath her. Her pussy lips were swelling against the tightness of the crotch band of her panties and she could feel a slowly rising moistness in her vagina. It was a warm slippery feeling that excited and tormented her and she flexed her inner thigh muscles to relieve the lewdly growing sensation.

"You're tense, Sis. Relax and enjoy it." Her brother whispered hotly behind her ear. He was bending over her, his body close. She could feel the heat of his breath on the nape of her neck, sending a prickly sensation down her spine to where his hand was now massaging the smooth rounded cheeks of her buttocks under her panties.

"Do you think this is right?" she asked, surprised how low and sexy her voice had become.

"Does it feel good?" Her younger brother asked, ignoring her question.

"Oh, Ned, it feels great, but... should we be doing this?"

The boy laughed and shifted behind her, taking his hand away.

"Okay, now just relax. Don't move, Sis," he said in a soft, hypnotic voice. "Just let your mind drift and enjoy the feeling."

It seemed forever before she felt his hands on her ankles, massaging them and moving them around. He pulled off her shoes and began massaging her feet as his voice continued in a low singsong way, "Just relax, total relaxation. All muscles relaxed, just relax and feel good, just relax nice and easy, relax." He went on talking with a hypnotic tone as Kathy felt his hands moving up her legs, moving over her calves and on up to the knee and to her thighs! Kathy felt her vagina swell again as she felt him pushing the hem of her dress up and massage her soft inner thighs in strong young hands.

With an ease that surprised her, he spread her legs gently apart and the band of her panties tightened up between her thighs and she felt one lip of her vagina slip free and the elastic legband of her panties were tight on her clitoris and so aroused and excited her she had to fight against the temptation to move her buttocks beneath his teasing fingers.

Her mouth was open, parted, and her eyes closed as she felt his fingers lightly teasing the insides of her thighs. She still had her stockings on but, in another few inches, he would be above the stockings and touching her bare flesh. Could he see up under her dress? Was he looking now and seeing where she was staining her panties wet from so much excitement? Could she stand much more of this teasing? What, she wondered, was she doing? She had never felt like this before. What did Ned think he was going to do to her, his own sister. Was it really possible?

He spread her legs wider, forcing them apart with his strong hands. Then, taking his hands away, she felt him slowly push her skirt up around her waist. It caught under her and pulled the crotch band of the soft nylon panties excruciatingly tighter between her open thighs. Now the band slipped, bit, deeper into her cunt slit and, as he bunched the dress around her waist, she felt the band slide into the deep crevice between her buttocks.

God, she thought, I'm so exposed and hot! I must look like one of those awful girls to him!

The thought seemed to explode in her

mind and her buttocks in sudden, abject surrender writhed, grinding down into the rug as she let out a little moan of helpless delight and felt the panties slipping back and forth over her now distended and throbbing clitoris. Behind her, she heard the rustle of her brother's shirt and from his movements, she knew he was taking his clothes off.

Ned had looked down at his married sister with a lopsided, triumphant little smile on his face. There she was, her dress bunched up around her waist, her bra undone and her back naked, her legs wide apart, her stockings, garter belt, and panties still on, and she was undulating and grinding her buttocks around, lifting them slightly and flexing her muscles. The panties bit deep into the crevice of her buttocks, exposing the white, rounded cheeks of her ass that quivered and hollowed as she writhed hotly in her drug-induced excitement.

"That's it, do that more," he whispered as he crouched naked over her.

The prickly surface of the rug excited her all the more and she moaned, "Oh, God, Ned. We shouldn't be doing this. No, not at alllllllll."

"Doesn't it feel good?" he asked in a smutty whisper.

"Ohhhhhhh," she said as she ground down on the rug with her groin, thrilling to the feelings that were pulsing through her body. It was wrong what she was doing, very wrong and the 'wrongness' of it excited her more than she had ever been before.

Then suddenly Ned was lying next to her and her body stiffened and tensed as she felt his hard young cock pressing against her side. Her own brother's cock pressing against her! And it felt so hard and huge and evil! Before she could react or say anything, his hand was once again on her buttocks. This time he was bold and brazen, pushing their soft quivering roundness down hard into the floor and imitating her lewd grinding movement. "Oh God, Ned, don't, please don't," she whispered, pleading, her voice shaking in helpless fear of what her sub-conscious knew was now inevitable.

He paid no attention to her, only continuing his teasing grinding motion until she felt her hips voluntarily responding. She couldn't help herself any longer. All thoughts of her husband and morality drifted from her mind and she moaned in helpless surrender, her eyes still closed as she rolled limply over on her back and lay with her legs spread invitingly apart and one arm over her eyes. She heard herself hiss out the words and, as she said them, she felt as though obscene magical flames, flames of sweetness and heat and desire were licking hungrily at her cunt. "You can do anything you want to me!"

Ned grinned again in triumph and propped himself on one elbow and looked down at his older sister. Damn, he thought, she is built. Jesus, what a hot little body! Wonder if her husband fucks her shitless when he's home?

He stared at her trembling body, his grin loose and depraved. Lying on her back, she was naked to the waist and her breasts were full and beautiful, like two snow-white ripe melons with little shadows under each one. Her nipples were small and pointed and hard, revealing her excitement. The breasts were so perfectly round and formed and set off by her incredibly thin waist. Her rib cage jutted out in a tantalizing way and his fingers itched to hold her by the ribs and lick and bite her nipples. With a cold-blooded voyeurism, he took his time, drinking in all her beauty and savouring it.

Her eyes closed, her mind whirling in drugged surrender, Kathy was relishing her feelings of lust and brazenness. She had never been so hot before in her life, had never felt so lascivious and evil before. And... with her own little brother! Languidly, her body tingling with lewd delight, she shifted her hips, tilting her pelvis up so that the crotch band of her panties pressed deeper and rubbed harder into her now passion-drenched vaginal slit. An insane idea was in her mind and the more she thought of it, the more she liked it. She felt as if her open cunt were boiling in a cauldron. She had to get satisfaction. Being lewd had only served to flame her desires. A mad little smile played around her lips as she still kept her arm over her eyes. "Treat me," she whispered, thrilled by the lewdness of what she was going to say, "Treat me like you did those girls. Just like you had picked me up tonight in a bar."

"You'd like that, huh?" Ned breathed in her ear.

"Yes!"

"Want me to do everything to you?"

"Yes!"

"Tell me you want me to fuck you, Sis."

Kathy took a deep breath and hissed out the words. "I want you to fuck me!" The obscene words coming from her own lips thrilled her and she felt his hand close over her cunt still covered by the wetness of her panties and a spasm of pure lust swept through her. Ned was going to take his savage good time with her. Something, an evil desire, swept through him. When he got through with his newly married young sister, she would really know what it's like to get the life fucked out of her. She was his now for as long as he wanted to enjoy her.

He looked at her flat stomach as smooth as silk and at her panties barely covering her desire-flooded pussy. The band between her legs was now a thin slit, revealing her soft, curling pubic hair and one swollen lip of her vagina. By tilting his head ever so slightly, he could see just a slit of her vaginal wall, red and glistening with excitement. In a few minutes, he would have her naked and spreading her cunt wide for his pleasure. He was going to treat her like a whore, bring her down to her true level and show her what she was really like. A twisted grin was on his face. This, to him, was what it was all about, breaking down women's egos until they begged to be fucked and groveled at his feet and pleaded for more. Once aroused, women were all alike. And he loved it.

Roughly, saying, "Okay, I'm going to give it to you," he pulled at her dress bunched around her waist and his sister flexed her knees and lifted her hips free of the floor as he pulled the dress off and threw it across the room. "Like a whore!" he said in a hoarse voice, the words thrilling her. "Like a God damned whore!"

And she moaned with delight as he bent over her, his thumbs under her white silky panties as he pulled them down. She jumped with delight as she felt the electric shock of his wet tongue on her stomach as he pulled her panties lower, revealing the soft resilient triangle of her pubic hair.

Ned pulled the panties over her rounded hips and down to her ankles where she kicked them off. Then, her eyes smoky with passion, she bent her knees again and slowly, lewdly, with her younger brother breathlessly watching, she spread her legs wide.

Ned looked with a lust making his face hard. Her cunt was now naked and, with a thumb and forefinger, he slowly spread the hair-lined lips of her pussy wide while she moaned and ground her buttocks salaciously down into the rug, the softness of it just tickling her exposed anus. Ned looked at her cunt spread wide, red and moist, ready for him to do anything he wanted. Bending closer, he flicked the tip of his tongue over her clitoris and Kathy reacted violently. "Agggggghhhhhaaaaaa!"

Her arm was flung away from her face and she looked to see Ned's face poised expectantly between her thighs and she pushed her hips up and saw his tongue flick out again and she felt the soft hot wetness lick at her cunt and clitoris and she felt she was going to explode with desire. He was on his knees, his back and tight bare buttocks facing her. She touched his thighs and he turned his hips so that she could see, with an audible gasp, his erect penis.

It was so big! Bigger than even her husband's and she had thought that Don's had been huge! Big and thick and swelling with a lustful excitement, the foreskin pulling back to reveal the smooth rubbery head. As she watched, half frightened yet aroused by the maddening white-hot thrusts of his tongue into her willing and begging cunt, Ned began squirming along the rug, that huge cock moving closer and closer to her head and face and, with another gasp, her mouth!

With a deft movement, he swung one leg over her head and was straddling her face upside down, still licking at her cunt. She moaned aloud as he slowly sunk his tongue into her excitedly throbbing pussy and wiggled it around. She closed her eyes and rolled her head around as she felt the first deep stirrings of an orgasm come rushing on. No one had ever done such a thing to her before and she had never even dreamed of the searing exquisite pleasure of such a thing.

She opened her eyes to see his huge cock looming in front of her face. She felt like she was in a cave, a cave made of human flesh and nowhere for her to turn. And, as she watched, Ned lowered his hips so that the head of his cock brushed rubberlike against her lips.

This was something she had never done with Don even though he had hinted at it. The thought of it had always repulsed her. Now, with her own brother's tongue sliding in and out and all over her cunt, teasing her, driving her on, pleasing her and building the momentum for an orgasm, she didn't know how she felt. He was treating her like one of those awful girls he had told her about and she felt a lewd thrill. The tip of her tongue licked slowly over the thick head of his cock and she smiled with the thrill and knowledge of power over him as she saw his cock jerk tighter in front of her face.

As if answering her in kind, Ned looped his arms around her thighs and pulled her legs wide apart and buried his face deeper in her defenselessly spread cunt, his tongue darting in and out and wiggling against the soft glistening walls of her vagina.

Kathy was galvanized, twisted, searing inside, into a lewd response. She arched her back and tilted up her pelvis and felt, with a little moan of joy, his finger probing for her anus. Her head thrown back, her hands up before her face, she seized his throbbing prick in her fingers and opened her mouth wide. With a slow thrust of his hips, Ned shoved his cock into the warm moisture of his married sister's mouth and Kathy felt it hot and hard on her lips. Her mouth was open wide, her lips fitting tightly around the massive mushroom head, her tongue twirling and tasting a drop of his cum on the very tip and liking it.

With a malicious sweet slowness, Ned took

his mouth from her open convulsive cunt and began fucking up and down into her tightly locked lips, enjoying the sensual feeling of having her helpless under him. Whenever he thrust down, Kathy's lipstick rimmed lips would go white and roll in as she held tight and tried not to choke. As he pulled out, her lips would balloon out as she sucked with all her might and fought to keep his swelling prick in her mouth.

Ned pumped up and down with a slow lewdness, his hips moving as he looked down at her cunt in front of his face, her thighs held wide apart and watched her undulate and writhe in a silent begging for him to lick her more. That crooked cruel grin split his face savagely as he began to increase the tempo and strength of his thrusts, thinking, for a wild moment, he would just cum in her mouth and leave her own body hot and helpless. With a snarl, he changed his mind. Kathy had always been the "good one" in the family and tonight he was going to show her just how "good" she really was.

He rolled off her with Kathy scrambling, clutching for his cock like a demented animal deprived of its dinner. He gave her a straight arm and knocked her over on her back where he leaped on top of her. The impact of his strong young body caused her eyes to blink and lose focus as she felt the aching pain spread through her rib cage and lungs as her breath left her body. He seized her arms by the wrists and forced them back up over her head, making her breasts thrust up tantalizingly.

With his knees, he forced her legs apart and stuck his cock down along the open slit of her cunt. Kathy, with a dreamy smile, eyes closed, squeezed her thighs closed around his lust-hardened young cock and felt it big and hard and throbbing in the soft flesh between her thighs and felt her wet cunt slipping over the side of his shaft and she worked her pelvis, rubbing up and down the rock hard shaft, teasing and exciting herself.

She suddenly felt a pagan atavistic thrill: she was alive and almost being fucked by her own brother; more than that, more than the lusty lewd thrill of doing something wrong, committing infidelity, she was doing something that all of society, from time immemorial, had condemned. She was doing something that everyone secretly wished and desired and feared! She grinned up at her brother's face hovering over her with the guilty knowledge that they were being carnal in the most sinful way. Incest! The very thought of the word made her feel as if the floor reeled and rolled under them and it seemed as if a roaring fire were in her groin and she twisted and writhed her naked body licentiously around under her brother. She was panting excitedly now as she spread her legs as wide as they would go and undulated her hips up, feeling her cunt slip and slide up and down the full length of his virile young cock.

But Ned wasn't ready to fuck her yet; he had more in store for her. She was not yet animal enough to satisfy his sadistic ego. When he was through with her, she would never forget this night, she would never be the same. He grinned triumphantly. Few men wanted to realize how lewd women really are and how easy it was to get them into a state where they acted like, and became, complete whores. The more you made them feel like depraved sluts, the better they liked it. And it was all so ridiculously easy if only one had the guts to do it.

Slowly, he forced her wrists together so that he could hold them with one hand. His other hand freed, he pried it under her back, arching it even more, her large lovely breasts spilling upward and now in front of her face. He let his tongue lick. and tease around the distended nipples of her breasts while she breathlessly watched. She tilted her head forward and he slid her wrists underneath so that they made a knuckled pillow and her face was tilted even closer, her chin rubbing against the soft resilient flesh of her breasts.

She watched in mesmerized lust, her eyes

clouded and out of focus as he sucked and bit a nipple just a few inches from her face. She moaned, her mouth open as she felt streaks of searing pleasure course through her body and explode in the depths of her belly. Her orgasm seemed like a cauldron churning, bubbling, soaring upward, filling her until she thought she would burst. With his chin (she could feel the stubble of his beard scratching her sensitive flesh) he tilted the nipple even closer to her mouth. Incest! The word seemed to hiss through the air as her hips undulated and her cunt convulsed and twitched against the shaft of his rigid cock. It was not enough to fuck and suck her own brother, it was not enough to act depraved, she must love her own body, raise her pagan lust by exciting herself even more in front of him. The insidious delight of further perverting herself seized her in iron talons. She would do anything and everything he demanded and she hoped he would demand that she do everything.

Closing her eyes, an expression of utter lust coming over her face, changing her into a wanton bitch ramming and grovelling-for more pleasure, her tongue slid slowly out of her open mouth and slowly licked her own nipple.

"That's it, Sis!" Ned gasped, "Suck it!"

He pulled his hand free while Kathy, her hips still pumping enticingly, let her hands stay

under her head while Ned cupped her large breast in his free hand and gently pushed her wildly distended nipple into her open mouth. Kathy's wet lips closed over her nipple in a babylike sucking motion while Ned tilted his head and nibbled on her other nipple while watching her blissful expression as she mewled and writhed under him. Shifting his hips, he placed the head of his cock on the lips of her vagina and she strained upward and outward, eager to have him fuck her.

With a sudden savage thrust of his hips, he rammed the head of his prick through the thin covering of soft curling pubic hair and on into her cunt with a quick wet slurping sound, stretching the warm wet walls tight and round and Kathy opened her mouth and let out a low moan of pure pleasure as she felt the walls of her vagina being stretched to the point of pain, a pain that was oddly pleasing and exciting.

Then, just as suddenly, he was withdrawing, pulling out and leaping to his feet, jerking her to her feet by one arm. Nothing was said as he dragged her through the apartment, the only sound being the two of them panting as they stumbled into the bedroom and he spun her around and threw her sprawling on her husband's and her bed where she lay on her back, her legs spread wide, the slit of her cunt wide and glistening in the midst of the soft sparse pubic hair between her thighs.

Ned was kneeling on the floor, tearing at his backpack and sleeping bag, drawing out lengths of rope he used when camping. Crouching over the foot of the bed, his teeth bared as he breathed hard, he looped the rope around one ankle and passed the rope under the bed. Bringing it up on the other side, he lashed the end around her other ankle then pulled the rope tight, dragging her legs helplessly wide apart while his sister winced and moaned under the pain of having her legs split so wide apart and tied down. Looping the rope, he crawled up the bed and bound her wrists to the upper posts so that she lay helpless, tied in a spread eagle position while her younger brother kneeled between her legs, his face twisted in passion.

With a guttural snarl, he fell on her and plunged his virile young cock deep into her wide-open cunt and Kathy screamed as loud as she could while Ned attacked her brutally, fucking her helplessly bound body with all his might. Kathy thought she was going to pass out as he tore at her vagina, banging the blunt head of his prick cruelly against her cervix. She thought she would go mad from the pain and rendering until she felt her orgasm coming again, mingling with the pain, becoming the pain, the pain becoming a wild irresistible pleasure that mounted until she felt the top of her head was going to burst off. "Fuck me!" she gasped, "Fuck me, fuck it, fuck me, Nedeeeee!"

Their naked flesh smacking together in a lewd sensuous sexual dance, glistening with sweat, bucking, grappling, undulating and slapping together with Kathy moving as much as the cruel biting ropes would allow, Ned gasped, "I'm not through with you yet, you hot, married little bitch!"

"Aaaaagggggghhhhhaaaaaaaaa!" The grinding moan seemed to come from her very soul as her body twisted up in catatonic pleasure. In a superhuman effort, she lifted the two of them off the bed, only her head and heels touching as she was held tense, her inner thigh muscles quivering crazily in the throes of her orgasm. She came again and again, twitching, convulsive, her mouth open and her eyes showing white as her body twitched and trembled from head to foot. "Oh God, Nedeeee... I... I'mmmmm c... c... cummmmning!"

And her body collapsed under him, her bones turning to warm butter as she felt his cock still ramming into her cunt that was still spastically spurting, the tightly clenching little lips seeming to grip the shaft of his prick in a hotly locked death squeeze.

With a snarl, Ned pulled free and crawled up her bound body, straddling his knees on either side of her full rounded breasts and seizing her head in his hands and pulling it up and forward. His fingers were entwined in her hair and Kathy's eyes went wide as she realized what he was going to do, the wetly glistening head of his cock looming in front of her face. "Ned!" she blurted, "No! No, n... oooooo! Cum in my cunt, darling... cum in my cunt... !"

But her voice was instantly cut off as he shoved his huge cock in her mouth, choking her as she tasted the heat and wetness of her own vaginal juice. The cock fucked in and out of her mouth with a lubricated ease, growing in size with his excitement. Despite her pain, Kathy felt herself growing excited again as her younger brother increased the rhythm of his strokes, his hips pumping his cock in and out until he threw his head back and bellowed as his prick swelled in her mouth, filling it completely. Then... she felt hot sperm spurt from his cock and hit the back of her throat and she swallowed as he came again and again, filling her mouth and ballooning her cheeks out as she swallowed to keep from choking. She swallowed the warm slippery liquid again and again as she felt his body slowly relaxing, listing to one side, his hands becoming limp and falling from her head as he moaned in wild, satiated delight.

With a newborn lewdness twisting her

hips, she sucked on his deflating cock with all her might, determined, in a lubricious way, to suck him completely dry. She could feel his loins trembling in fine spasms as he fell from her, his cock slithering from her lips, a thin rubbery strand spilling out to lie glistening on her breast as he fell heavily to lie next to her.

She lay trapped, naked and lewd in her marijuana inspired lust, her hips pumping as she writhed against her bonds, wanting to fuck more, wanting to fuck the night away. "Ned!" she gasped, looking at him wildly, hungrily.

Ned propped on one elbow and grinned at her. "Hot again, huh? Want to get fucked some more?" "Ned!" she hissed between clenched teeth as she heaved and twisted her buttocks.

"Let me hear you say it, married sister!" he said maliciously.

Kathy closed her eyes and her head thrashed back and forth to blot out the thought of her husband, Don. "Fuck me, fuck me more!" she said, her voice hard and low.

Ned got up and stared blearily around the room. "Must be something here." He stumbled from the room into the bathroom while Kathy raised her head and wondered what he was doing, crashing around in the bathroom.

The answer was in front of her in a moment. He came from the bathroom slowly, that same old sardonic smile playing on his lips. He had something in his hand, concealed behind his body.

He brought it slowly into view. It was a hairbrush! Her very own hairbrush – the one with a large, thick handle. "This'll do," he said, getting on the bed and kneeling between her wide-split legs, "Until I decide to fuck you again."

With a moan, Kathy let her head fall back, her mouth open, tensing her legs and flexing her knees as much as she could as she rolled her buttocks under and thrust her cunt open for her brother to do whatever he wished.

Chapter 3

Sitting alone in her kitchen, her eyes despairing and vacant, Kathy drained her cup of coffee and liquor and put her face in her hands and sobbed.

The utter animalistic way she had behaved, the sheer joy with which she had taken to depravity, the lust she felt searing through her body, had been undeniable. She had loved every lewd second of it. Had she stopped there, she might have had some feeble excuse. She had been drunk and drugged. There was no doubt in her mind that Ned had taken an inhuman and unholy advantage of her. Nor was there any doubt in her mind that Ned, her brother, was some kind of satanic monster, that he was close to madness, that he would someday do something for which society would kill him. There was no stopping the demonic impulses that drove him to such reckless acts. Nor did he seem to feel any remorse or guilt afterward.

Just the opposite was true. His excesses only led him to wilder fantasies. He seemed to have Kathy hypnotized. She could not resist him. And that was the real horror, for she realized, with a growing revulsion and sense of doom, that he was her brother, her own flesh and blood and she was like him! She loved the revolting things he made her do, she gloried in them!

They had fucked the night away until, with trembling fingers weak from so many orgasms, he had untied her and she had collapsed into a deep exhausted sleep.

A jarring pain had pulled her back to consciousness. It was morning and hard sunlight streaming in through the windows made her eyeballs ache and Ned was on top of her again, his erect young cock again pushing into her sperm-flooded cunt. She didn't believe her body could ache so in every bone and her cunt felt raw and sore. "Ned," she moaned, "Please, please, no, not now."

But her feeble pleas were lost as he began to fuck her brutally and she could feel her body greedily responding to it. Above her, Ned held her close and whispered in her ear. "Ever been fucked like that?"

The evil pleasure of hearing him talk to her like that only added to her growing excitement. "No!"

"Don ever that good?"

She hesitated, her body stiffening as she thought of her husband. Oh God, she loved him!

"Don got a cock like mine?" Ned persisted, fucking her harder.

She fought against answering. She would do anything he wanted except deny Don! She fought, her teeth clenched as she felt her hips beginning to pump back and she wished to be tied down again and have him do whatever he wanted. "Answer me!" he demanded harshly, grinding his cock head deep up against her cervix.

She winced with the pain and her lips parted. "N... no!"

"No what?" he grated.

"No, not like you." She said it with a sigh, the lewd admittance and betrayal exciting her all the more. God, she thought, I'm going to cum again! He's going to fuck me to death!

"Has he got a cock like mine?" Ned demanded, crushing her in his arms as he forced his hand down the length of her back and his fingers found the deep crack between her round buttocks and his forefinger pressed against the tight puckered entrance of her anus.

"Ahhhhhh!" a sigh of pure pleasure and depravity came from deep within her as she felt the finger press as his cock sawed in and out of her again, passion-wet cunt.

"Answer me!

"No. No!" And something inside of her grew, an orgasm as she hungrily kissed his open mouth and ran her tongue slipping around his lips. "Nobody has got a cock like yours!" she gasped, wild with desire.

"Not even Don?"

"No, you're better!"

"Better than Don?"

"Bigger and better and fuck me, fuck me, Ned!" And he had, the two of them having another orgasm and falling into exhausted sleep to wake when it was dark out.

Sitting at the kitchen table, remembering it all and feeling a mixture of hate and remembered excitement, her vaginal walls wet with desire and her mind full of self loathing, blinded by tears, Kathy staggered to her feet and blindly felt for the bottle, pouring and spilling the liquor on the counter top and finally, in a desperate attempt to numb herself from the sickening thoughts and remembered images, she drank from the bottle, tilting her head back, some of the drink spilling and snaking down her cheek and throat as she choked and pulled the bottle away and gasped for breath.

"Oh God!" she choked as she put the bottle down and covered her mouth with her hand and slid along the counter top until she came to the sink where she retched over an over again.

She found her way to the bedroom where she fell on the unmade bed. She lay there thinking how the whole house was a mess, how she seemed to be going to the dogs, and she thought of killing herself, committing suicide, rather than face the fact that she was as depraved as her brother, Ned.

Brother? She shook her head. He was more than a brother, he was her lover. She loved the way he had treated her and knew if he should come back, if he should be alone with her ever again, she would find herself helpless before his insane and vile will, that she would do anything he asked.

There seemed no way out of it. The thought of facing Don again, of putting her arms around him and kissing him, of getting into bed naked and making love with him after what she had done and said, seemed impossible. She had betrayed Don at Ned's command and did so many times while he stayed with her.

Lying on the bed, exhausted, Don's letter crumpled in her hand by the force of her misery, she tried to will herself to think of all they did together, of all Ned had done to her.

She had liked feeling abject and conquered in front of him, rising that night and cooking his meal which he silently and greedily ate, then, throwing his napkin down and getting to his feet, she followed him back to the bedroom, clad in nothing but a transparent negligee that he had demanded she wear, feeling sexy and trembling with anticipation at what he would ask her to do. He stood in front of the full length mirror that was attached to the bathroom door and looked over his shoulder, grinning, his lips thin and cruel. "Come here."

She obediently stood in front of the mirror, looking at her voluptuous body, her nipples pressing through the flimsy material, seeing the soft triangle of pubic hair showing. She wasn't drugged and hadn't anything to drink now. She was cold sober, rational, and yet, she still felt her vaginal lips swelling and the walls of her cunt pulsating with a wild wetness. His hard strong hands were on her shoulders and he was forcing her down, down on her knees and she kneeled in front of him, looking at her obedient body in the mirror.

Ned stood with his legs apart. He didn't have to say anything; she knew, he was her brother. With trembling fingers, she unzipped his fly and fumbled for his hardening cock and took it from his pants, excited all over again by its size as it swelled in her hand and she watched her fingers slowly pull the skin back and saw her mouth slowly open and watched, helpless, loving her humiliation and degradation, as he slowly pumped his hips forward and his cock slid into her mouth and she saw her lips grow thin and tight around the thick full shaft and felt the delicious taste in her mouth.

His hands entwined in her hair and his breathing was becoming excited and his face distorted as they both watched, standing in front of the mirror with Kathy kneeling at his feet, her hands guiding his cock into her mouth. "Fingerfuck yourself while I watch!" he hissed.

Again, she knew what he wanted and one hand slid down over her breasts, down over her slim waist and pulled up the hem of her negligee as she shifted on her knees, spreading them wide apart and her fingers felt the pulsing wet slit of her cunt and she teased and caressed her clitoris into a wild swelling that made her pump her buttocks lewdly as she sucked on his cock and watched herself doing this incredible wild thing in the mirror as he sawed in and out of her widely ovaled mouth with an increasing depth and tempo and she saw her hand moving rhythmically over her own cunt and then, with a shivering thrill, plunging one finger into its soft wetness up to the knuckle and fingering it back and forth in time to his thrusts into her mouth.

Then she forced in another finger as she felt her heat and excitement mounting as she urged herself, and Ned, on to still another orgasm.

Then, as unpredictable and inexplicable as ever, Ned shoved her away with a cruel grimace, stepping back and putting his prick back into his pants and zipping them up. Kathy, on the floor, naked from the waist down, looked up at him full of fear and frustrated desire.

He sauntered to his sleeping bag again, grinning at her over his shoulder. "Just wanted you in the right mood for some more fun," he said, bending over the bag and unfolding it and looking. He straightened up with a camera in his hand, checking it for focus and film.

Kathy had tried to compose herself as she got up off the floor and sat on the edge of the bed, brushing her hair from her eyes. "What are you going to do?" she asked, knowing what he had in his mind and hoping against hope he wouldn't say it.

For an answer, Ned snapped in place a flash cube and aiming the camera, tripped the shutter and the room exploded as if lightning had gone off just as Kathy folded her arms over her breasts. "Ned! No!" she called, blinded by the flash.

He let a low cruel chuckle come from his throat. "Come on, now you're getting shy? Get on the bed!" he demanded, pointing.

"Ned, don't make me do that," she pleaded, whining, finding an odd twisted enjoyment in begging him. She felt her desire building again yet she forced herself to fight it. "Please, Ned, I'll do anything, else. I've done everything you've asked."

"And you loved it," he said scornfully. "Look, Babe, get off that high horse you've been on for years. Face it, you're just like me."

She couldn't answer him, just looked at him with an imploring look, her hands and arms trying to hide her abundant charms.

Ned only sneered back at her. "Get on the bed. Lie down. You said you wanted me to treat you like those other chicks. Come on, lie down," he said in a menacing voice.

She felt her will dwindling. She had done

everything else she could imagine. Why not this? Why not pose like some common whore? Why not debase herself like she had heard of girls doing? Why not pose for pictures she had heard men got in Tijuana? Her voice was weak and her mouth dry as she asked, "W... what are you g... going to do w... with them?"

Ned wound the film and snorted. "What do you think? I'm going to show them around to my friends. Sell them if they're any good."

"Ned!" she implored, her face wild. "You couldn't! I'm your sister. I'll do anything you say but please don't do this to me. You could ruin me!"

His face like a clenched fist, he leaned forward and asked, "How?"

"P... people seeing me." With a helpless wave of the hand, she stammered, "I... like that! My God, if they got into the wrong hands! Our parents! Don! My God, do want to ruin me? Us?"

Ned looked thoughtful. At the possibility of endangering himself, he grew responsive. He drummed his nails on the side of the camera. "Okay. Maybe you've got a point. But, in return for my not taking any pictures, you've got to do exactly what I say."

Kathy heaved a sigh of relief and clasped her hands together. "Anything, anything you want!"

He swaggered in front of her then put the camera down. "That's better. First, we're going to have a few drinks and then blow some more grass," He chuckled and pinched the nipple on her breast, "All to get you in the right frame of mind. Then, you'll put on a dress with nothing on underneath and we'll go out."

She tensed again. "Out? Where?"

Ned looked down at her with raised eyebrows. "Where? Where else? To a movie, naturally."

"A movie?" she asked, again dumbfounded by his sudden change of pace.

"Yeah," he said, stretching languidly. "Coming into town I saw a couple of skin flicks were playing at a drive-in. We can take your car." He left the room, heading for the kitchen to pour the drinks, calling back over his shoulder. "By the way, you got any bread?"

"Bread?" she asked, wondering why he wanted bread when he had just eaten and just rejected several slices she had made for him. "There's some toast on the table," she called, getting to her feet and wondering what dress would please him. She had one miniskirt she was saving to wear for Don. Forlornly, she thought, that's all dead now.

A wild peal of laughter came from the kitchen. "Are you ever square. I mean money, loot, folding bills."

"Money? Yes, I have some. Why?"

"Good," he called back above ice rattling. "Then you pay. The movies will be my treat for being such a nice guy."

They drove to the movie in silence, Kathy driving with extra caution after having had two drinks and smoked more of Ned's marijuana. Again, her mind was befuddled and, instead of thinking clearly, instead of trying to talk to Ned and make him see and understand what he was doing to her, instead of talking ration and reason, she found herself silent, staring ahead, thinking of what it felt like to be naked under her simple miniskirt and how it gave her an odd smutty feeling. And then, drug induced, her mind reeled back over the obscene things she had done with her younger brother and she found herself ravenously hungry for more.

Ned, relaxed, slumped in his seat, pulled up her miniskirt and smiled down at her bare thighs. They were long and rounded and he liked seeing them spread wide apart. Kathy's hand came slowly down to pull the skirt, up around her waist, down. She did it with a firm movement, "So near the toll booth. I have to pay."

Ned looked up to see they were only one car away from the booth on Kathy's side. He laughed and playfully flipped the dress back up. "Leave it up. Give the guy in the booth a cheap thrill."

Nervous, looking down, Kathy drove up to the booth and put her purse in her lap and nervously pawed for her change purse.

The attendant on duty, a young kid, looked down into the car and caught his breath, wetting his lips. The young girl in the car was wearing a low cut dress and he could see almost to her nipples as she bent over her purse, her breasts full and milky white and jiggling as she hunted and desperately ticked her teeth and tongue. He leaned further out the window and saw her naked thigh and, his eyes bugging, her naked hip and a full lovely curving outline of her buttock.

Finding the money, Kathy thrust several bills at the attendant, lying forward to do so, and allowing him to see one ripe bullet-shaped nipple a dark red. He leaned far out the window, repeating the license number silently several times. He and his friends might find that worth looking into later on, when he was off duty.

Kathy was intent on parking and, when she had shut off the ignition and turned out the lights, she turned to Ned. "I feel..." Her thought was left unfinished as she looked down and discovered he had his cock out and it was erect. It stood in the dark of the car thick and obscene and Kathy felt a sluttish thrill of the pleasure it had driven her to: flights of sheer sexual ecstasy she never dreamed existed.

Ned was rough and crude as he lunged at her and kissed her on the mouth, forcing her head back and pinning her arms to her side as his hand rammed between her legs and his fingers roughly probed her vagina. "Ned!" she said, twisting her head to one side. "Not here!"

"Why not? Everybody does at a place like this. Nobody knows we're brother and sister. That's all in your head." Brutally, he forced her head and kissed her wantonly on the mouth, his insistent fingers caressing her swelling vaginal lips.

Kathy let her body go limp and, with a lewd thrill running through her body like warm molten plastic, she spread her legs wide and slid forward on the seat, allowing one of his fingers to slide into her moist cunt. Her hands groped for his cock.

Ned pushed her away and grabbed her by the shoulders. "Get on top of me," he said in a low tense voice.

Kathy looked around. "People will see," she whispered.

"So what?" he growled. "Come on, damn you, I want it."

"How about on the floor or in the back seat?"

"No!" he demanded. "Come on, I want

you to ride me."

Brushing the hair out of her eyes, a hateful lubricious thrill of captivity again surged in her body and she swung around, facing her brother, putting her arms around his neck and straddling his lap, a knee on the seat on either side of him. She closed her eyes, feeling her vagina being spread wide by his fingers. And then, with a shiver and a low moan, she felt him rubbing the massive head of his cock up and down her wide-spread slit. My God, she thought, I'm wet already.

His free hand pulled her dress high up around her waist and Kathy was naked from the waist down, kneeling on the car seat, her lovely full buttocks spread wide, a dimple in each cheek. ANYONE CAN WALK BY THE WINDOWS AND SEE went wildly through her mind.

And indeed, a couple in a nearby car looked and saw her, moving to position herself, her arms around Ned's neck, her eyes closed. They turned from the skin flick on the screen, which was tedious at the moment, explaining why it was going to be exciting later on. If people have the choice between seeing a movie and watching the real thing, they'll take the real thing every time. The couple crowded to one side of the car as they watched her bare buttocks and thin waist maneuver themselves in place. Then they

saw her throw her head back and sigh as she slowly sank down on her partner's lap.

Inside the car, they gave out twin moans of pleasure as Kathy slowly lowered her loins, feeling the hard head of his cock spreading her pussy lips open, making her cunt bulge out on the sides as she felt his ramrod shaft rise inside of her, filling her up. She jerked and sighed as he thrust his hips upward, shoving more of his prick into her. She felt its passage smooth and lubricated and loved the stretched painful feeling that she knew would rise to a wild pleasure.

She began to undulate up and down; slowly at first, savouring every delicious minute of her movement. She felt free and wanton and she slowly gyrated her hips in a slow teasing circular motion ending with a sudden breathtaking thrust down in which she felt his cock ram its full way home and Ned let his head fall back as he moaned, "Do it, all the way, all the way, Babe!"

She withdrew slowly, climbing in a squirming motion back up the length of his prick, using her thigh muscles and groin to make her cunt lips squeeze, slip, and contract all round his throbbing cock.

With his hands, he began pushing her skirt up. Kathy couldn't care; the ride, the undulating up-and-down motion was a sexual roller-coaster she was on and she felt a lewd and overwhelming orgasm building in her loins. "I'm going to cummmmm," she crooned.

Her hips began moving like they were on stainless steel springs as she looked down and, in the dark, could see the thick glistening shaft of his cock disappearing between her legs, stabbing into her cunt. Ned had pulled the dress up so that her back was completely bare now and the couple in the next car began caressing one another and necking as they watched her gyrations grow more frenetic and abandoned.

Ned was forcing her arms up now, her breasts hanging free and ripe. They were swollen with desire as he put one nipple in his mouth and sucked while Kathy, eyes shut, moaned and tossed her head from side to side. She was indifferent to anything around her. The only thing that mattered was her brother's virile young cock fucking in and out of her cunt and her orgasm which was on the verge of exploding inside of her. With wild unseeing eyes, she took in the car that pulled up next to them, full of teenage boys. It was the booth attendant with his young friends.

"They're looooking," she whispered, "They're watching, and I'm cummmmminnnnng!"

Six teenagers with the attendant craned their heads and watched, their young cocks growing hard in their pants as they saw the woman naked, flinging off her dress over her head and saw her with her head thrown back, her back arched, her hands around her partner's head as she fucked and writhed up and down, faster and faster, her heavy full breasts thrust out and upward, jiggling and undulating in her frenzy and, through two panes of glass, they saw and heard her cry of passion as she tensed and shook all over. They watched, breathing hard, as they saw her collapse and saw the man struggling brutally to get her off his lap. She disappeared from sight, falling over on the driver's seat and, for a moment, they couldn't see anything but the looming figure of the man.

"Shit!" one of them said. Then as they watched, they saw one of her legs thrown over the back seat then the other, placed by the man, up on the dashboard and they saw the man fall on her with a wild force. "Jesus, he's fucking her now!" one said.

"Yeah, let's get out and see."

"Look at him go!"

"Yeah, maybe we can get some of that pussy too!"

"Yeah! A gang-bang!"

"I can't see too much."

"Look at him fuck. He's going to fuck the life out of that broad!"

"I can't see too much. Let's get out."

The words stung them all into action. They

got out full of giggles and whispered warnings to be careful and quiet. They crowded around the windows of the car, much to the annoyance of the couple in the other car, and peeked in.

They saw Kathy naked and wanton, her head hanging off the front seat, her huge, rounded breasts cupped in her hands as her finger tips teased her distended nipples while her legs were thrown wide apart and up high. Ned had her by the hips and was sawing his thick long cock in and out of her with a savage abandon. He saw the dark heads bobbing outside the car and grinned like a wolf as he fucked his sister harder and harder.

Kathy, her body being battered into a corner, her breasts lurching and jiggling with every heavy cruel thrust, got sight of the bulging eyes looking down at her and wished – wildly, insanely that they would all get in the car and fuck her into unconsciousness.

Then, Ned came with a wild roar, pumping his hot young sperm deep up into her hotly clasping cunt, filling her up with a wild desire that boomed into another orgasm for her, shaking her body in a continual earthquake and making her feel weak and near fainting from such searing pleasure.

They lay limp, breathing hard until Ned roused himself and pulled up into a sitting position. Instantly, the boys retreated to their car. They sat, horny and frustrated, talking among themselves, trying to work up enough courage for one of them to go over and talk.

Kathy pulled herself up, full of fatigue and sudden shame. Hastily, she groped for her dress and pulled it on over her head, staring straight ahead at the screen. With a moan, she closed her eyes. On the screen two naked women were on a bed, a blonde and a brunette and they were caressing one another with their eyes closed. She had completely forgotten they had gone to skin flicks, hadn't even looked at the screen once.

She jerked erect, catching her breath as she heard a tapping on the window on the passenger side, next to Ned. She looked to see a boy crouching next to the car. To her amazement, Ned casually rolled the window down and said, "What do you want?"

The boy, the attendant, shoved his head in the window and leered at Kathy, his greedy young eyes mentally undressing her. Then he grinned at Ned. "No offense, man, but, like, we saw you and…" with a smirk he nodded at Kathy, "her."

"So?" Ned seemed so unconcerned.

"Well, you know." The attendant looked at Kathy again, his smile slack and his lips wet. "Like, if it's all right, you know, how about letting us have a little?"

"What?" Ned laughed. "You and your friends?"

The attendant looked a little sheepish. "Well, yeah. I mean, you know... it looked so good."

Ned shifted to look at Kathy for a long moment. His face was in a cruel composure and he seemed mildly amused. Then he turned to the attendant again. "You want to fuck her?"

"Do I? Oh, man."

"And your friends?"

"Yeah. Why not?"

Ned looked back at Kathy and tapped his fingers on his lips. "Why not?"

"I got a friend in a camper a few rows back. We could use that." The attendant was all action, grinning and hurrying away to make plans.

Kathy looked at the carfull of leering kids on her left and, without a word or hesitation, she started the car and backed out, the tires screeching. She drove fast and recklessly out of the lot, her brother lurching from side to side and yelling, "Hey, take it easy. What the hell are you doing? Watch it, for Christ's sake!"

Kathy went roaring out of the lot, down the road kicking up dust and swerved onto the highway, barely missing an oncoming car which swerved as its horn wailed in the night. She whipped down the highway then swerved to the curb and slammed on the brakes so hard Ned was thrown up against the windshield.

She turned on him fiercely, her eyes shining in the dark. "Now you get this straight! I'll do anything you want, anything you say just so long as it is done with you. I'll act like a whore, a dirty slut, do you hear me, if you want me to, but I will not, I repeat, I WILL NOT DO THAT FOR ANYONE ELSE! Is that clear?"

Before Ned could react or answer, she went on, her voice rising, "And another thing. I'll do any filthy thing you want, but ROD WILL NEVER KNOW! If he ever finds out, if you should ever even so much as drop a hint, so help me God, I'LL KILL YOU! Is that clear?"

Dumbly he nodded then let out a low laugh. "Well, big sister is finally liberated."

Kathy looked to check the traffic then snapped her head back to him. "Don't talk to me!"

They drove back to the apartment in utter silence, the two of them staring ahead and not looking at each other as they entered the apartment. Kathy went directly to her room, slamming the door, leaving it unlocked as a gesture of defiance. She stripped quickly, took a long hot shower then toweled her body until it felt good and clean and dressed in a cotton nightgown, she stood by her bed and clicked out the light.

And listened.

No sound came from the living room except low music from the radio. She saw light coming in under the door and got into bed softly, closed her eyes and wished for sleep. Later, she was making a conscious effort to will herself to sleep. Then she prayed for sleep.

Then she lay staring up at the ceiling. Kathy was going through those long night hours when there is no one to turn to. Her anguish and shame tore at her soul for long hours with only the clock ticking beside her, acting as a metronome to her agony.

Far into the night, the low music played on in the living room, punctuated only by Kathy's sighs and mumbled commercials on the radio. A restlessness enveloped her. She sat up and squinted at the clock. It was two o'clock in the morning. She lay back, resigned. If HE should come through the door, she could not stop him. She was exhausted, red-eyed, yet she could imagine fucking him one more time.

The endless music and silence in the next room piqued her curiosity. She slipped out of bed, tiptoed to the door and opened it a crack. She could see Ned lying on his stomach on the couch, sound asleep.

It is part of Kathy's character, part of

the goodness in her that made her suddenly relax and step into the room as she had for so many years when they lived at home and she had stepped into his room, clucked her tongue and proceeded to clean up after her wild young brother. She clicked off the radio, went to a closet and got down a blanket and tenderly draped it over him, pausing to see that he had an angelic smile on his face.

She couldn't help smiling, remembering him when he was the angel of the family, when he was her wild laughing kid brother, when she used to tease him and love him so. And now, her face twisting, she realized the love was now a secret obscene thing; an attraction that she loathed and loved, gloatingly, greedily, both at once and at the same time. The more disgusted with herself she became, the more excited was her mind and her body.

Kneeling beside him, thinking of what they had done at the drive-in and what Ned had wanted her to do with all those other boys, Kathy grimaced as she fought against the rising tide of her lust. Twisting her hips, she could feel the slippery moistness in her vagina and wildly she thought of undressing him, licking and sucking his prick while he was asleep and of what could have happened had she gone to the trailer, the camper? What would it have been like, she wondered, her hand stealing under her cotton nightgown and stroking the insides of her thighs as she looked down at his face. Could I do that, she wondered. Could I go in there, be naked with them? Cocks all around. Do whatever they want? Could I? She straightened up and shook her head and turned out the light.

She stood for a minute, listening to his deep regular breathing in the darkness, thinking: Could I? What would it be like? Could I? Still, it wouldn't be so different. No. I can't think like that!

She fled the room almost as if chased by some ghostly watchdog. She huddled in her bed, curling up and shivering. The thought of those six boys excited her and she tried not to admit it. She fell into a deep troubled sleep murmuring "No," and "Never," over and over.

Chapter 4

Seven more days until Don came home. Then it was six. Then five. And four. Three, two one. And she was wide awake, opening the drapes in the bedroom to allow the first rays of morning sunshine in and, today, Don would finally be home.

The time had passed so fast and Kathy had tried to cut down on her nightly drinking but found it impossible. To compensate, she became maniacal about cleaning the house and having everything neat and in its place. She made endless trips to the Laundromat and spent hours scrubbing and polishing the floor. She sat, drinking, planning the home coming meal in her mind with endless changes. She polished what silver they had for three nights running. And tried to decide what she would do.

And, now, she stood in her nightgown, rubbing her eyes and looking at the morning sun over the city. In the year since Don had seen her, she had changed. Her face was somehow older with the beginnings of hard lines on her cheeks and an odd look in her eyes. It seemed sad at times. Other times it seemed to smoke with a repressed emotion. A kind of masochistic smile on her lips when she looked that way.

And Don had changed. Driving to the airport, she didn't know what to expect. Rather, she imagined they would see one another and rush into each other's arms. Or, she would see him and rush at him, that old feeling for him real when she was in his presence. Somehow, it wasn't at all like that. She had stood in the airport lobby, listening to the great whoosh of incoming planes and the rising, screaming whine of the great jets taking off and absently glanced around and saw him, Don, standing looking at each other.

They walked towards each other slowly, each intent on the other, each knowing that the other had changed. They walked toward each other like people who had dated once years before. Kathy's smile was warm and friendly "Hi."

Don stood looking down at her. His face was older, harder, thinner. Also, he seemed taller. "Hi."

"You've lost weight," she said.

"So have you." And, for the first time, he smiled, crow's feet appearing at the corners of his eyes.

"Welcome home, Don."

"Good to be home, darling."

"Are you all right?"

"Of course I am," he scoffed. "How about yourself?

"I'm fine now that you're here."

"Same here." He stepped forward to take her in his arms.

"Don?" And her hand shot up, stopping him.

"What?" he asked, squinting.

Kathy hesitated, opened her mouth, closed it and, as glimmers of tears danced in her eyes, she said, "I love you."

"And I love you, honey," he said as he took her in his arms and kissed her.

"Don?"

"Yes?" he murmured, fighting for her lips.

"I need you!"

Don gave a satisfied little laugh and hugged her tight. "And I need you too. Boy, did I miss you!"

"I mean I really need you!" she sobbed.

"Okay. I'll never go away again."

"Promise?

"Promise."

They left the terminal arm-in-arm laughing. Don drove home with Kathy snuggled close beside him, trying not to think of what she had done in the car.

Don insisted on carrying her into the apartment and put her down, taking off his tie and coat. "Wow. I don't believe it. Fix me a drink after a nice long kiss."

She had stepped into his arms and felt his kiss and sensed his lack of ardour. Something, a little indefinable something told her that all was not right. Fearful that she might, in some way, some reserve, give away the all consuming lust she had had for her brother, she rubbed her hips against him and brushed her thighs back and forth.

Now, it was he, who pulled away. Her first numbing fear was that, in some way, he knew about her and his brother-in-law. If Ned had told him! She stood frozen by fear, waiting for the scalding word to come out of his mouth. Incest!

Instead, he waved a hand and said, "I'm sorry, it's me. Look, a lot has happened and it was a long flight and I'm dead on my feet. How about that drink?"

She exploded in relief. "Of course! How would you like it? On the rocks with a little soda?" That was the way he used to like his drink.

Don looked thoughtful. "Better make that neat."

"Neat?" She looked at him questioningly.

He nodded. "Neat."

He looked so different to her standing in the middle of the room with his hands on his hips. Thinner, yes, but changed around the eyes and mouth. Even his attitude was different. She smiled and spun from him, saying, "One neat scotch coming up." In the kitchen, she poured herself a drink that was pretty generous. To cover up, she poured more scotch in his glass.

They sat on the couch together, holding hands, eagerly telling each other any and all big news they had. Don said he was on leave for a month then only had to report back for processing on his discharge.

"Will you be going back to your old job?

Have you written the advertising agency?"

Don looked down at the floor, took a big drink, then let his head flop back on the couch. "No, I haven't."

"Are you going to call them?"

Don looked vague. "No, I'm not."

"Why?" Kathy bit her lip.

"Well," he gave a little laugh, "I don't think I want to be in advertising any more."

They both took quick drinks and Kathy took their glasses to the kitchen and poured bigger drinks. Sitting next to him, she looked at his face and knew he was troubled, that he had come to some new understanding of himself. Having gone through the problem with horrendous consequences, she was sympathetic. Could she, for a few moments, forget her own deep problems?. "What do you want to do, then?" she finally asked.

He shrugged. "That's it. I don't know." He gave a little laugh. "I don't have the slightest idea what I want to do."

"Maybe you want to go back to school?" she asked hopefully.

He made a face and took a deep drink. "Nuts. All those long hairs running around and rioting and mouthing off about a lot of causes they don't even understand." Don was up on his feet and it seemed like he was letting out some of what was bothering him so Kathy sat quiet as he talked on. "I'm too old for that crap. Listen, to them, it's all a game. They're over here and bad mouthing and thinking they've got the problems of the world licked and they don't even know what it's all about."

He was striding about the room, drinking, staring off, shooting glances her way while he talked on. "There they are and there I am. There I am in my little chopper, taking off, doing it from the manual, doing just like in training only I'm not in training, I'm in Vietnam and my chopper is loaded down with wounded men. Men blown half apart by land mines and men with their faces blown off by booby traps and kids bleeding, their life blood spilling out of them."

He paused for a moment, drained his glass then went on. "Sometimes I was so loaded I had stretcher cases lashed to my landing pontoons. Sometimes I had such a load of wounded, I couldn't get too much altitude and I'd have to fly between the hills and I'd look out at those guys and see them looking at me with those eyes and sometimes those bastards up in the hills would fire on us."

He paused and Kathy got up to take his glass. "Honey, I'm so sorry."

Don raked a hand through his hair and scoffed. "I'm sorry. Doing a job like that day in and day out can warp your perspective."

Kathy shuddered. "I'll bet. You've seen

too much suffering."

Don gave a harsh laugh as he followed her out to the kitchen and stood watching as she mixed the drinks. "It's more than just that. It's the whole God damn country. Corruption everywhere. In the towns, it's all black market, whores, and dope."

Kathy looked at him. "Really?"

"The whole place is miserable. There isn't one decent person in that whole stinking country. Sometimes, I just wished I could put it all down and walk away from it. Just say the hell with it."

"What did you do to keep from going crazy?"

Don took his drink, took a big swig then tilted his glass in a little ironic toast. "Well, booze, for one thing."

Kathy cocked her head. "For one thing?"

Don looked at her seriously. "Yes. Pot, for another. Don't look so shocked or upset. Everybody over there smokes it. The stuff grows wild all over the place. Everybody does it. And with good cause. Keeps you from going nuts and busting the place up."

"I... didn't know," Kathy said, wondering if she should tell him she had smoked it, wondering if she should tell him anything about Ned having been there. "You never wrote me about it."

"It's something you don't write home

about." With a shrug, he grabbed the bottle and walked back into the living room, sprawling on the couch and saying, "Let's have some music or television or something."

Kathy followed him. Her mind was a mixture of emotions and conflicting thoughts. She had hoped he would be calm and strong and take charge of their life and be someone she could lean on; someone she could love and trust and perhaps, someday, confide in and tell all of what was burning in her soul and groin. She needed to tell someone what she was going through and that someone had been Don. Now, here he was; restless, disillusioned, bitter, drinking, unsure.

The fact that he had confessed he had smoked pot in Vietnam had a double effect: first, a relief in that he had done it too; a way, in fact, of admitting she had done it with Ned and a way of opening up the subject. Yet, at the same time, there was the realization that, if he had smoked pot, he had felt the way she had and he could have found it easy to find willing girls.

"And what else did you do?" she asked, sitting next to him and beginning to feel the blissful relief and relaxation from the booze.

Don looked mystified. "What else did I do?"

"To keep from going crazy."

"Over there? Oh, the usual. Crap games,

card games. I told you about the boozing. Movies, when we could get them. And the dope," he added, waving the bottle a little drunkenly.

"And what else?"

He looked at her owlishly. "What do you mean, what else?"

Kathy tried to look coy. "No women?"

Don gave a humorless laugh. "Naw."

"Come on, you can tell me."

"Say," he said, pausing to drink, "What kind of guy do you think I am?"

"Like every other husband far away from home and lonely, and upset," Kathy said with an expansive and tolerating wave of the hand.

"No, not me," Don answered, looking down at his glass.

"I hear those Vietnamese girls are pretty cute. I've seen them on the news. Some of them are knockouts," she said, teasing, moving closer and letting her hand stroke his thigh.

"Yeah, some of them are, but those aren't the bar girls. You can't get near those girls."

"Yeah, but I bet you didn't have any difficulty getting near those bar girls."

"No," he said, shaking his head. "Oh, a couple of times we fooled around. Couple of the guys used to make out, but I never did more than buy them a couple of drinks."

Kathy threw her hand to her mouth and laughed. "I bet. Come on, Don, I love you. Are we going to have secrets from one an other?" she asked, amazed at her own excitement and lack of guilt. A wild thrill ran through her. She felt like Ned. It was a lewd thrill that made her lean forward, her lips wet and parted, her eyes half closed, her breast brushing against his shoulder as she whispered, "Come on, tell me about it."

Don burst away from her, getting to his feet. "All right," he said, waving his glass. "So I did. Just once. That's all. I was drunk and lonely and hadn't heard from you for a long while and I met this girl and went and did it."

"I wrote you every day," she said, a little defiantly. Even though it appeased her conscience a little to know that he too had been unfaithful, it hurt her pride and she felt a pang of jealousy creep into her being.

"The mail was held up lots of times and I'd get a whole lot of letters at once," he alibied. "Anyway, that's no excuse. Honey, forgive me. Try to understand. She meant nothing to me and I was lonely and I didn't even enjoy it."

Triumph, a coarse and wicked kind of triumph came over her. With a lewd smile, she knew she had him. She got up off the couch, put down her drink and walked to the bedroom door. Turning to him, she began to languidly unbutton the front of her dress. "Was she any good?" she asked in a low voice.

Don, still standing in the center of the room, watched her with narrowing eyes. "No, just a girl." He thought of young Diu and her more knowing sidekick, Xuan. Hell, it was another country, another *world!*

"A prostitute?" she asked, slipping one snowy shoulder free and revealing she was wearing a black half-bra that barely caught and contained a rounded and billowing breast.

He drank from his glass, watching her with greedy eyes over the rim. "Yeah, she was a prostitute." She slipped her other shoulder free and stood with the dress falling past her tight slim waist and catching on her beautifully rounded hips. "What did she look like?" she murmured.

He grinned sheepishly. "Oh, all right. Say, what are we talking about her for?"

Slowly, provocatively, she shifted her weight from hip to hip and Don felt his cock give a jerk as he saw the red of one nipple working its way loose from her bra and the dress slipped lower on her hips, revealing she was wearing a scarlet garter belt. "Was she good looking?" she persisted.

He was now looking at her body, at her

inviting, bare midriff that undulated as she moved her hips in time to the music. "I already told you," he said, finding his mouth suddenly dry.

With a slow, shimmying movement, the dress slithered to the floor and she stood in stockings, high heels, black bikini panties, red garter belt and a flimsy half bra that her heavy ripe melon-breasts were bouncing out of. "Did she look as sexy as me?" she asked, her voice low.

Don gulped at his drink, draining it and standing looking at her loveliness. Her long tapering legs seemed to curve all the more as she raised one and bent the knee across her body, seeming to hide her private loveliness but only exposing one taut cheek of her buttocks as the panties rode up into the deep crevice. With an enticing look, she whispered, "Why don't we go in here and talk about it?"

Slowly, she turned, revealing the full impact of her pert buttocks half naked and alluring, and walked into the darkness of their bedroom. Without a word, Don watched her go, watched the rhythmic rise and fall of the naked cheeks of her buttocks. Hastily, he poured himself another drink and gulped it down and followed her into the bedroom.

He found her on the bed, on her back. Her huge breasts had flowed out of the bra, her nipples red and distended. Her breasts seemed higher, jutting upward with the help of the bra and she lay with one leg bent and across her body. Slowly, she straightened the leg and spread both of them. He was standing at the foot of the bed, looking at her body, his eyes zeroing in on her crotch where he could plainly see the imprint of her vagina on the tight black band and several tiny curling strands of her pubic hair sticking out. And, as he watched, wiping the back of his hand across his mouth, she let her hips undulate ever so little.

With a cry, he was on the bed and crashing on top of her, fully clothed, his mouth on hers and his hands running up and down her body. He was shocked and surprised with the intensity and abandon of her response. She ground her hips up against him and her hands pawed at his clothing, trying to get it off him while her open mouth kissed him and her hot tongue ran wild in his mouth.

They writhed together, as he felt her hip bones jutting up and his hands ran wild over her body, rudely grabbing her breasts, her buttocks, then, with a guttural cry, cupping his hand over her cunt and feeling it hot and swollen and moist under the panties. He rolled off her and was surprised how quickly she sprang to help him out of his clothes. Stripped to his shorts, his cock bulging beneath them, it was Kathy who fought his hands away and forced him to lie back while she pulled them down, his cock flopping into sight and waving erect.

She threw his shorts on the floor then propped herself above him on her arms, smiling down at him. Tantalizingly, she let her breasts skim over his chest, her nipples being prickled by his chest hair. "Was she good to you?" she asked in a whisper.

Passionate, drunk, he was bewildered.

"Was who good to what?"

"The girl, the prostitute," she said with a smutty smile. "What did she do to you?" As an incentive to answer, she lowered her body until her hot silky stomach was just touching his cock. She rocked slowly back and forth and then up and down, applying just enough pressure to tease him and roll the foreskin back. Don groaned. "Oh, wow, it's been so long. What difference does it make what she did?"

"None," she cooed. "But I want to hear what she did to you?" she asked, putting her stockinged knee between his legs and forcing them apart. Slowly, she let her weight come down on him, her breasts bulging in front of his face.

"The usual," he said, running his hands down her back and snapping her bra loose and letting his hands go on down to where they touched the top of her panties. Slowly, he tugged them downward as she lifted her hips to allow him to do so.

"And what's the usual?"

"You know."

"No, I don't. Tell me."

"You know."

"Tell me!"

"They... they did what most of the girls do."

"What's that?" she asked with smokey eyes, feeling her excitement mount. It was almost as good as being with Ned. She would get him to tell her what the girl had done to him and she would, in a kind of subjugation, do the same to him.

"Well, they sort of make love to the guy."

"How?"

He closed his eyes. He was being driven mad by her writhing body. Half drunk, having confessed to sex he thought: what the hell. "They sort of put. Well, they used their mouths."

"Ohhhhhhh." It was a low exclamation of understanding and pleasure that came from his wife. Slowly, she began slipping down the length of his body, her mouth licking, kissing, biting. She paused to nibble at his chest, sending a crude feeling of lust scorching through his groin. She made a wet trail across his stomach, pausing to probe her tongue into his navel, then slip on down to, with a jerk, and a moan, he felt the hot wet tip of her tongue flick across the end of his cock. He raised his head with a dazed expression and saw her over his cock, her mouth open, her tongue out, her eyes closed and her face radiant with lust. While he watched, he saw her wet her lips with her tongue and slowly open her mouth wide and take his cock in her mouth where he felt a rubbery wet softness. Slowly, her lips taut as a rubber band, she began to bob her head up and down.

His head fell back and he let out a moan as he felt her begin to expertly suck as her mouth and tongue moved over his rock hard shaft. It had been awhile since he had had a woman and his body writhed convulsively and he fought against a raunchy pumping of his hips which he knew from experience would heighten the feeling yet wasn't something he should do with his own wife.

His wife!

The thought hit him like a thunderbolt. Here she was, acting like a Vietnamese whore, asking him what they did and then doing it! Somehow, it wasn't right. Yet, it felt so good and it was fun. But, with Kathy? Sweet, innocent young Kathy?

The thought that his pent-up passion was getting out of hand and he would, like she was some common whore, shoot off in her mouth, suddenly become appallingly real. Frantically, he tore out her head, pulling her away with all his strength.

Kathy got her breath and brushed the hair out of her eyes, whispering softly, "What's the matter, darling?"

"Nothing. Just getting kind of excited, that's all," he said, gasping.

She squeezed his cock with her hand and said, "Isn't that the whole idea?"

"Yeah, but I might cum!"

She tilted her head and looked down at him with a strange sexually provocative smile. "So?"

"Well... it's not right."

She pursed her lips and smiled mockingly. "Not right? What did you do with that girl? Didn't you come in her mouth?"

At her use of the word, "come," he stiffened. She never used to talk like that. She had changed. As he remembered, she was always responsive, but shy and passive. Drunkenly he tried to remember if she had ever gone down on him before. But, his lust couldn't be denied.

"Well," she asked again, "Didn't you come in their mouths? Didn't you like that?"

"Yeah," he admitted, "But that was different."

"How? Did they do something that I don't do?

"No! I didn't mean that. I mean it was

different. That was her job."

"And this one," she said, squeezing his cock again, "Is my job."

She bent her head again and he felt her hot wet mouth close over the mushrooming head of his cock and felt her warm slippery tongue slide around with the tip licking over the entrance to his prick, trying to tantalize the hot male juice out. He moaned with delight but couldn't let his wife behave in this way. He reached down and tried to lift her head with both his hands.

Kathy responded by locking her arms around his widespread thighs and sucking with all her might, her head bobbing as fast as she could.

"Kathy!" he gasped, "Stop it, stop it, God damn it!"

They fought, with Don pulling her hair until he was afraid it would rip loose, then trying to wedge his hand down to push her face away. His fingers felt the diamond hard erection and her lips swooping down and touching his fingers. His shaft was wet and a low lewd thrill ran through him as he felt her lips slip down and suck on the tips of his fingers. One of her hands coming from under his muscular thighs, seized his fingers and guided them and encouraged them to grip the shaft of his cock and, with a low, sensual moan, he grabbed it and pulled the foreskin further back, feeling her lips and tongue exploring new contours of his prick. With a greedy lust, he stroked the skin back and forth as he groaned and moaned with pleasure while below, his wife increased the rhythm of her sucking.

With a shock, he felt her forefinger probing the tight crevice of his buttocks, teasing in to find his tiny puckered anus. Nothing but the most depraved Vietnamese women ever did that! Of course, he expected it from them, demanded it, even. And now, at home, his wife's forefinger was flicking back and forth, sending shivers up and down his spine as she sucked with a wild abandon on his cock!

He was going wild, nearing a monster orgasm. It was not right to do a thing like that with your wife, he told himself and he fought with a renewed effort, using all his strength, not caring if he hurt her or not, only concerned with stopping what they were doing. They tossed back and forth and he fought, trying to pull out from under her and, as he did, he felt her finger pop into his anus and he gave a yell. Despite himself, despite all his struggling, he found his hips pumping in rhythm to her sucking and he writhed and pumped and, with a desperate effort, rolled over so that she was under him.

The lewdness of their pose sent rockets exploding in his skull. He was on top of her, his cock still in her mouth, her arms still locked around his thighs. With a wild hoarse cry, he began fucking her in the mouth as though it were another cunt. He couldn't help it, it felt so good and the whole thing was better than any Saturday night whore he had ever heard of. Her finger was slipping deeper into his anus as he thrust in and out and he fought with her again, turning over once more so that she was on top of him. Then, with a wild cry and wild thrust, they twisted and tumbled off the bed and fell to the floor where he landed on top of her.

She was sucking harder than ever, holding on to him with all her strength and all reserve, all morals were gone and abandoned. He was going to fuck the shit out of her. He pumped in and out of her mouth with all his might while her finger sawed in and out of his anus and her lips were like a vacuum stopper around his cock, sucking hard.

Now he was fucking into her roundly ovaled mouth viciously, pumping in and out with all his might, carelessly banging her head down on the carpet as he suddenly threw back his head and yelled, "Aggghhhhaaa!" and pumped white hot sperm deep down into her hungrily! He felt her sucking still and looked down to see her cheeks ballooning between her legs. He saw his cock swelling with each explosion of cum and saw her swallowing hard and sucking for still more and, as her finger gyrated in his anus, he felt he would never have a sweeter orgasm ever and the sight of her greedy sucking sent secondary spasms coursing through his body and he came again and again, gradually collapsing and falling to one side as she turned with him, still sucking his deflating cock. Soon, he was flat on his back on the floor, relaxed, his eyes closed, feeling her over him, sucking the last bit of cum from his soft cock then licking it clean. Then she stopped and he felt like falling asleep.

He raised his head and saw her walking quickly from the room, her buttocks twitching up and down. Jesus, he thought, and I haven't even fucked her yet!

She came back quickly with the bottle and two glasses. She knelt beside him, her breasts naked and tempting as they quivered, and poured two drinks. "How was that?" she asked, handing him a drink.

Don drained his glass and handed it back, gasping for breath. "That... that was out of sight."

Kathy looked pleased and leaned over him, one nipple near his mouth. "I'm glad. What else did they do?"

"Who?" he asked, knowing full well what she was talking about.

Insinuatingly, she rubbed the nipple across

his lips. "You know. I'm hot. That was good. I'll do that to you again."

Despite his fatigue, he felt a tremor of excitement grow in his prick. "What else did they do to make you happy?" she asked, persisting.

He looked at her, doubtful. "Aren't you mad or jealous?"

She drank and smiled down at him. From her eyes, he could tell she was getting smashed. "No," she said, slurring the word. "Oh, a little, but I understand. You were far, far away from home."

"Yeah," he said with a smirk, taking another drink from her. What the hell, he thought, she's excited because I'm home. "Some of them were pretty good," he said, slipping into the plural without realising that he had now admitted to screwing around with several Vietnamese ladies of the night. He had just about decided they both would get drunk and make some more love. Get drunk. Get laid. Get drunk again. Get laid again... Hell, there was a pattern to it that seemed familiar somehow

"What did they do?" she asked with her eyes glazed from more than booze.

"Oh, the better whorehouses had shows," he said with a bragging kind of nonchalance.

"What kind of shows?" She seemed to be eager to know. It was almost as if talking about such things meant as much as the actual thing. "Well, strip shows and shows with girls making love and shows with girls making love with animals."

"Animals!" she squealed. "I don't believe you!"

"Honest. I saw one girl with a dog and another girl with a donkey. Honest. I talked to the girl with the dog and she said no man could ever satisfy her again after she had a dog. Can you imagine anything so depraved?"

Kathy squirmed closer, her hand playing with his prick. Against all he wished, he found it growing harder under her gentle ministrations. "What kind of a dog was it?"

"Big German Police dog. Belonged to the Saigon police department."

"And what did it do to the girl?" she asked breathlessly.

"It fucked the life out of her. In her ass," he added softly as though an afterthought.

Kathy's heavy sigh and strange excited expression was the first real sign to him that something was wrong. He fought with his alcohol befogged mind. She was never this way before. Something had happened. What could be the truth dawned on him in a frightening way. Just as he had been busy with whores in Vietnam, so she could be busy with men back at home!

He started to prop himself up on his knees but his wife had gotten up and was standing over him, pulling her scanty panties off as he watched. She stood, clad in nothing but her high heels, stockings, and garter belt. Swaying from drunkenness just a bit, she stepped, placing a leg on either side of his head and Don threw his head back and looked up.

The sight inflamed his lust again and he felt his cock swelling painfully blood full and erect. She stood above him with her hands on her hips, her legs apart and he looked up her long legs and could see the glistening slit of her cunt buried in her dark pubic hair and the tight deep crevice where her plump buttocks met. Slowly, as he watched, her hips began to gyrate and her legs spread apart. He saw her hands coming down and caressing her pubic hair and he saw her forefinger slide its lubricated way up and down the length of her cunt and she began to slowly spread her legs, kneeling as she did so. Above was her slim stomach, now heaving with desire. His mesmerized eye traveled on up, up to where he saw her great breasts jutting out, almost obscuring her face. Between her cleavage, he could see her chin tilted, her head thrown back.

His hands began caressing the insides of her calves and ran on up to stroke the insides of her thighs and, as he watched, he saw her fingers form on the lips of her vagina and slowly pull it open and wide. The glistening red walls of her cunt were now visible to him. As he watched, his cock now ramrod hard again, she began to slowly gyrate. The sight was too much for him as he saw her cunt twitch and gape, one of her fingers running in and coming out wet and her buttocks moved in a rubbery way, expanding enough for him to see a glimpse of her anus.

He wanted to lick her cunt; something that he had never done. Certainly not with the Saigon bar girls – only little Xiu had been the exception to that rule. No telling what kind of diseases they had. Yet, he couldn't bring himself to do it, even as she was bending lower, spreading her legs wider while her fingers toyed with her throbbing little clitoris and slipped in and out of her cunt.

He pushed her away and got to his feet and she fell back, her breasts jiggling obscenely. "Do you want me to suck you some more?" she asked. Her reaction was strange, for he thought he saw a shivery, sexual thrill run through her body, making her tremble. There was an odd look in her eye, like she wished for him to make her suck him again.

Grabbing her by the wrist, he pulled her to her feet and spun her on the bed where she sprawled and spread her legs. She lay there, her arms thrown behind her head, her breasts heaving with passion as she rolled her buttocks under and started her hips in a long slow pumping as if some invisible cock was fucking in and out of her.

Don watched, aroused, as she squeezed her moist cunt together between her soft thighs and trembled with lust and desire. She writhed and undulated before him, her hands coming down to cup her breasts. He crawled on the bed, panting, kneeling between her legs and lying on top of her, his cock held away from her cunt. He felt her long legs wrapping around his body, pulling him in while her buttocks squirmed under him, yearning for his prick. A wild excitement, spurred on by his drinking and her wantonness, made him say, what the hell, might as well go all the way. His mouth by her ear, he whispered. "There was this girl who showed me something once."

"What!" she whispered back, her voice excited and breathy.

"Tell me, I'll do it!"

He pulled away from her and said, "Roll over on your stomach." Instantly, she obeyed, lying flat with her head averted from him. If he could have seen her face, he would have found it glazed with a masochistic kind of lust. Instead, Don found himself gazing at her smooth firm buttocks. They were perfect and their sensuous symmetry made him stare down at them, fondle them, feel their warmth and soft rubbery firmness while Kathy moaned pleasantly. Lewdness had them both caught in its iron grip now as Don thought of steamy drunken days in at Mama Nu's where anything could be bought for a price and Kathy closed her eyes and dreamed of Ned and their night in the drive-in. Could she have gone back to that camper and been gangfucked by all those teenage boys? What was it Ned had said? Something about being liberated? Yes, she thought, her mind confused and boiling with lust, when I give in, I'm free!

"Spread your legs!" Don whispered hoarsely, feeling his cock grow erect and hard against his flat stomach. He watched as she obeyed, spreading her legs as far as possible while he crawled between them and looked down. Her buttocks were spread wide and the deep crevice between them widened until he could see the dark spot where her anus was. Below that, surrounded by sparsely curling pubic hair was her cunt, the lips spread wide so he could see the inflamed cherry-red walls all wet and inviting. She was crushing her clitoris down on the bed sheets and grinding away in a slow, deeply suggestive movement.

"Get up on your knees!" he commanded, his voice little more than a white breath of air. He watched as her buttocks rose in the air as she struggled to her knees, her legs still spread apart. Muscles and cords stood out as she rose obscenely on her knees, her ass held high with each cheek spread taut. Her defenceless puckered little anus was in full view. Never had Don seen anyone more naked or vulnerable as he saw her cunt with its vaginal lips swollen and spread. God, he thought, she looks just like a whore! His mouth dry, he said, "Reach back and spread your cunt with your hands."

He almost spat the word, "cunt," and he could see a visible reaction from Kathy. A shudder ran through her body and she reached, stretching her arms, around her tight young buttocks and felt with her fingertips for the lips of her vagina and slowly spread her cunt open wide.

With a roar, Don lunged between her legs, got to his knees and seized her hips with his hands, digging his fingers deep into her flesh and rammed his cock home as she moaned. He drove it as deep as it would go into her, feeling her cunt resist for an exquisite lubricated moment then plunging on in the full length of his shaft, feeling it surrounded by the feeling of warm, living honey.

He fucked her with abandon, slamming it into her, feeling his balls slap back and forth obscenely and seeing her with her head still on the bed, her face turned away from him, seeing her head jerk and recoil under the

impact of his thrusts. Below her, her breasts just touched the sheets and they quivered and jiggled as he fucked her, her nipples becoming distended and an excitement running through her body.

Kathy met each of his brutal thrusts by pushing back, eager to get every inch of his cock in her. His fingernails were digging deeper into her loins with each thrust and their pain was part of her humiliation and her humiliation was her excitement and pleasure. She felt an orgasm building in her and she longed for further depravity, for her brother to come back and to dominate her and force her to do obscene things.

And as she thought of Ned and what might have happened had she gone to that camper with those boys, her orgasm surged and welled up. "Oh God, darling, I'm cumming!" she panted.

Don threw his head back in wild abandon, gritting his teeth as he fucked as hard as he could and felt another orgasm coming on him.

"In the ass!" Kathy suddenly screamed, her voice harsh.

"What?"

"In the ass, fuck me in the ass if you want to!" she hissed, the words tearing across her vocal chords. "In the ass, fuck me in the ass like the dog!"

The thought drove Don mad but he was beyond control, beyond stopping. Kathy herself was driven wild by her confession of the lewd desire. A white light seemed to explode deep in her mind.

"I... I'm cummmmmmmming!" Her body tensed as she thrust upward. "I... I want... want... Aggggggghhhhhhhhhaaaaaaaah!" The sound seemed to come from the pit of her stomach as she came again and again, her cunt caught in tiny electric spasms.

Don came in her cunt, shooting a thin jet of scalding hot sperm so fast and hard he didn't realize it until he felt his cock thickening against the next burst. He came, taking a deep lungful of air and moaning as his body went limp under the massive pleasure of pumping hot juice into his wife's hungrily dilating cunt.

They collapsed, Don bearing down all his dead weight on his wife until he rolled off. Kathy, crawling exhausted under the covers, murmured something indistinguishable just before she fell almost instantly asleep. Don followed her, lying on his back, wearily reaching for and turning out the light. He lay still, catching his breath, feeling sleepy making everything fuzzy and incoherent.

His body flinched him awake and his mind was full of a yammering thought: she must have been fucking someone else. She was never like this before.

He lay thinking, not sure he wanted a wife who acted like a whore; not sure he liked his wife begging him to commit sodomy even though it was exciting at the time. It was not normal. He frowned up at the dark ceiling and thought a long time before going to sleep.

Chapter 5

The weeks that followed were spent in sightseeing in and around Santa Monica. Kathy found herself constantly trying to break through Don's increasing bitterness and depression. His confusion seemed to deepen and he refused, curtly, to talk of their future. "Plenty of time for that when I get my discharge," he would say, leaning his elbows against a railing and. gazing at the gorillas who sat in their pit, picking at fleas or lost in a stupid reverie.

Kathy, standing beside him, touched his shoulder lightly. "How long are we going to stand here looking at those apes?"

"I dunno."

"There are a lot of other animals to look at besides those hairy things."

"I like looking at them," he said with implacable finality, never wavering his gaze. They're kind of locked up the way everyone else is."

A look of concern crossed her face. "Why do you say that? We're locked up? We're free. This is America. They're on one side of the bars, we're on the other."

Don gave a secret bitter smile. "I know. Maybe we're all locked up."

Kathy grew silent. She waited patiently while Don moped, watching the great apes listlessly play with a car tire until he stretched and walked away. It was the same when she introduced him to her friends, proudly exhibiting her husband home from the wars. Don was polite and remote, usually sitting silent behind a drink.

He seemed to regard the war with a sorrow and scorn and seldom talked about it unless they were alone and he was drinking. Then, he would go off on some long, haranguing monologue. "I had a buddy over there. A big Aussie called Greg Bradley. Nice guy from Sydney. I'd promised to look him up if I ever got to his town. Greg was more than a buddy, he was a friend. I don't know why, we just got along. Talked a lot and he was pretty cool about everything. He didn't dig longhairs, neither do I. He didn't especially like listening to politicians, neither do I. He wanted to work for himself His old man was a druggist. He didn't want to do that when he got out. We had a half-assed idea that he might come over to Santa Monica and we'd do something besides hanging together when we got back."

Don would look down at his drink a long time before saying anything. Kathy had learned to sit quiet during these silences. He drank and went on. "We had our own apartment in Saigon that we shared. Greg had been seconded as liaison officer to our outfit and he'd been getting some experience with us before going back to his own Aussie unit. One day, we came back from some real rough runs. Three days straight. We were beat but we had to check out our choppers. It was a matter of professional pride, really. Like I said, we were both beat and seen enough guys blown apart so I suggested we flip and see who stayed behind and checked out both choppers. Greg agreed and I lost." A sad cynical smile crossed his face. "I won. I stayed at the base while Greg drove back to Saigon. Said he'd have a pitcher of martinis waiting, then we'd both go to Mama Nu's, a little drinking place we used to hang out at. Greg put the key in the lock, opened the door and got his head blown off. Booby trapped while we were away. None of the little bastards who worked for us had any idea who did it."

Yet it was more than just the readjustments of a returning soldier, more than learning to live with peace after a year of constant war. He was sullen and their evenings were spent in silent drinking while they sat in the living room, never looking at each other, having the television as a constant excuse. To the other servicemen they knew, husbands of friends of Kathy, Don was bored with their war stories and often rude.

They saw less and less of friends, their life becoming insular, their nights spent in drinking, their days spent in quiet desperation. Don seemed to avoid looking at her or talking to her as much as possible. During the day, he made excuses to get away from her. The car had to be taken in for servicing; he had to make trips to the base on vague business.

At night, they drank and. Don avoided their having sex again. Each night they went to bed and she was refused, Kathy's anxiety mounted. Since that first night, he had cut off all conversation about sex. Kathy cringed inwardly, feeling she had given herself away. Yet she couldn't help it. With a sickening feeling in her stomach, she had to admit to herself that she only lived for sex, perverted, filthy, dirty sex; that she would gladly, fervently, perform any and all obscenities that Don would ask her to do. With a shudder that made her wrap her arms around herself against a nonexistent cold wind, she thought she might be capable of performing any sex act that might be asked of her by anyone.

She knew she must be sick, she knew her desires and drives were not normal. Her body ached and throbbed for her brother Ned while her mind was revolted at her desires and lust.

They rose late every day, hung over, with Don irritable and non-communicative. He was sure, after the first night, that Kathy had taken a lover or lovers while he was away. The thought, added to his already existing feelings about the war, only deepened his rage. Nobody at home seemed to have any idea of what the war was all about and the thought of his own wife fucking her hot little ass off, acting like a common slut while he was over there trying to do something about all that endless misery, was too much. It seemed to him that nobody cared, that everybody had their heads in the sand and were busy enjoying themselves, that the peace demonstrators weren't so much interested in ending the war as they were in tooting their own horn and cause.

Over all of this, hanging heavy on his ego, was the feeling that his wife was not what he thought she was. Certainly not the girl he had left behind. What they had done in bed together was something he had done with whores, common prostitutes that he had paid. She had outdone the biggest whores at Yumyum's, the Saigon whorehouse devoted exclusively to oral sex. Was that any kind of a woman to be married to? Was that any way to build a future? No, she had been whoring around and he was going to bide his time, find the guy and then he was going to have his revenge.

Each day they arose late, Don taking a hot shower against his ramming headache, downing several Excedrin and a glass of foaming Bromo Seltzer then dressing and strolling out to the mailbox while Kathy showered.

Each day he went out, he caught sight of an old man in the yard across the street. Every morning, the old man pretended to be working but was always watching. Every morning, he seemed disappointed when Don came down the drive. Can he be the one? Don asked himself. Naw, too old. A good fuck would kill an old geezer like him.

One particular morning he came back into the house with an open letter in his hand. Kathy was in the kitchen, washing dishes from the night before and preparing a breakfast of black coffee and orange juice. "Hey," he called, "we got a letter from your brother, Ned. He says he's coming out to visit us for awhile."

There was the crash – an explosion – and tinkle of glass from the kitchen. Don ran to see Kathy staring at him with a white face, shattered glass at her feet.

"What happened?"

"Nothing. Slipped. My hands were soapy and it slipped. Let me see the letter."

"Look out, you're in your bare feet, you'll cut yourself," he said, alarmed by her pale appearance, the odd look in her eye and the way she walked through the glass, seemingly oblivious to pain or danger.

"Let me see!"

"Kathy, you're bleeding!"

"Let me see the letter!" she said in a strange wailing tone.

"Here, take it. Sit down."

He guided her to a chair, alarmed by the way she was behaving. She paid utterly no attention to her cut feet and her bleeding. He sat her down in a chair while her eyes raced madly through the letter.

She sat reading it over and over while Don ran to get the first aid kit and treated her cuts, pulling shards of glass from her feet. Her cuts sterilized and bandaged, he swept then vacuumed the floor then paused, caught his breath and looked at his wife. She was still as pale as a plaster wall, the letter, read many times over, in her lap, her face vacant of any emotion as she stared off, her eyes sad and resigned.

"Kathy, I've got to get you to a doctor," he said, concern in his voice.

"He can't stay here," she said in a small voice.

"Who? Ned? The hell with that now. Get dressed, I'm taking you to a doctor."

She looked up at him as if she hadn't heard. Her eyes seemed larger and darker than he had ever seen them before. And there was an odd unhealthy look to them. "I don't want him to stay here."

"Ned? Why not? He can sleep on the couch. Kathy, what the hell is the matter with you? Are you all right?"

She tried to smile and moved to get up, wincing as she put weight on one foot. "Ouch. Oh, that hurts."

"I know." All of his resentment was forgotten. The sight of blood, the thought and sight of someone in pain brought back feelings he had tried to bury and forget since coming back from Vietnam. No matter what he felt, he had been trained to help people when they were hurt. "Let me carry you to the bedroom where we can get you dressed. I've got to get you to the hospital."

"I'll be all right."

"You'll be all right when a qualified doctor can look at those cuts and get all the glass out. What got into you?" he asked as he picked her up in his strong arms and carried her to the bedroom where he put her on the bed and busied himself with gathering clothing for her.

Kathy lay back on the bed and closed her eyes, the letter crumbled in her hand. Once before she had lain on the bed, a letter in her hand: Don's. With a mighty effort, she tried to stir herself. "I don't know," she lied. "I felt so funny when I woke up. I felt worse when I was in the kitchen and that glass just slipped. I'm sorry."

"Forget it and get into these slacks and stuff." He smiled down at her. "You sure were weird about that letter. Walked right through the glass like it was nothing."

"I... I thought something was wrong with Ned. I just had a... funny feeling, that's all," she lied. She removed her robe, wearing only a bra and panties underneath. She paused and lay back, looking up at her husband with half closed eyes. "Don?" she asked longingly.

"What?"

"Make love to me."

"What? Now? The way you are?"

"Please. Now."

"Kathy, don't be crazy. You have a temperature?" He put his hand to her forehead and she seized it and licked the palm of his hand with her tongue. "Kathy!"

"Please," she implored, her voice breaking.

"It's so important. I need you. Make love to me, make violent love to me. Don! I need you! Please make love to me! Fuck me like you really mean it."

Don recoiled at the words. He looked down at his wife. Her face was so tortured, so serious. And there was that strange look in her eye. What was it? Had Don known, or had he even suspected the lust and agony Kathy was feeling at that moment, he would have been able to do something: a gesture, an act, a word. But, he had no idea. He busied himself with dressing her, treating her as a child, preferring to think her rantings came from the fact that she was hurt. He carried her to the car and whisked her off to the hospital, to the emergency ward where a doctor cleaned and treated her cuts, gave her an injection and prescribed some pills to relax and calm her and pronounced her cuts as not being serious at all.

They stopped at the drug store and Kathy sat in the car while Don ran in to have the prescription filled. She sat parked in the shopping centre and watched the people around her. They seemed so normal with such normal activities. Mothers and fathers with their children, teen-agers walking arm in arm, older people window shopping. All this, she thought, and Ned is coming. The letter didn't say when, just that he was on his way.

The letter was postmarked two days ago. He could be arriving at any time. What was she going to do?

Don broke her reverie as he got into the car, slamming the door and looking at her. "How're you feeling?"

She tried out a wan smile. "Better."

"You sure acted funny. All I said was I got a letter from Ned and you acted funny."

"I know." She took a deep breath and lied. "It's just that I never hear from him and he should be in school now. He was here awhile ago. Didn't I tell you?"

"No, I didn't know that. How was he?"

"Wild. Lot of things disturbing him. I worry about him and when you got that letter I had the crazy feeling something was very wrong. Silly. I'm so sorry."

For what seemed the first time in a long while, Don smiled at her warmly. "Forget it. Let's get home and give you this medicine."

Don was very attentive all evening long. He placed her on the couch and placed pillows behind her back and turned on the television and made and fetched her drinks. He even managed a simple dinner that he served her on the couch. Kathy was grateful for his attention even though she kept protesting she was all right and could manage for herself. The prescription, a tranquilizer, worked well and Kathy found herself being lulled into an artificial serenity by the combination of pills and scotch. She liked the lazy drowsy feeling they supplied her and drifted off to sleep, thinking of how nice it would be to take tranquilizers and make love. She curled on the couch, looking at Don with a sleepy-eyed look, smiling, murmuring, "Why don't we go to bed?"

Don nodded, watching the TV. "In a little while." His plan was to wait for her to fall asleep, cover her, turn everything off and go to bed alone, using the excuse that she needed sleep. He didn't have too long to wait and he sat smoking and drinking, pretending he was watching. television but really thinking about his wife. It was something more than just an affair. But what? Her behavior when he said he had a letter from Ned was odd. Weird, in fact. But why? He found Ned's letter and read it over. It was simple and short. Ned had been a visitor when he was in Vietnam. What had happened? Kathy called him wild and disturbed. What had happened and why did she wait until now to tell him Ned had visited? It wasn't like her to forget a thing like that. She had always been so fond of Ned.

"Fond." Sitting in the chair, tapping the letter thoughtfully against his chin, he said the word softly. He had heard of "stuff like that" in Vietnam. There was even the Okie kid, a real hayseed farm boy who said he had fucked his cousin and various farm animals. Don had always put him down as a bragging crackpot.

He shook his head and got to his feet. Nothing like that could happen here. He felt a little ashamed of himself for thinking such thoughts about his wife and brother-in-law. Hell, he thought, last time I saw him, he was just a kid.

He went to bed troubled, thinking. There was something very wrong with Kathy and something wrong with their marriage. He couldn't accept a wife who made love the way they had the last time. He had to talk to her. They both had to sit down and soberly talk over things. Maybe a visit to a minister or doctor would help. Something had to be done.

Something was done. It was done at three o'clock that morning. Don found himself stirring from a deep sleep by the persistent ringing of the front door bell. He got out of bed warily, drudging about on reflex, used to being called at all hours to fly his chopper on a mission. "All right, all right," he mumbled, stumbling to the living room and stopping sleepy eyed when he saw Kathy still sound asleep on the couch. The doorbell stabbed through the early morning silence and jolted him awake. He blinked and walked to the door, wrapping his robe around him.

"Who's there?"

"Me," a voice answered in a stage whisper. "That you, Don? It's me, Ned."

Don threw the door open and stood with a quizzical grin on his face. "Ned! What the hell are you doing?"

Ned came in. "Didn't you get my letter? I got a ride clear to Denver and got a plane down. How are you, you old son-of-a-gun?"

Don shook hands, taking in Ned's appearance sleepily. He had grown, becoming strong and rangy. Slimmer and not as tall as Don, but growing. And that crooked grin of his was familiar. To him, Ned always looked as if he had just come from pulling off some insane prank and was pleased with himself.

Don let him in, watching him haul in his gear and noticed his appearance was getting a little "farout". He grunted to himself, hoping his brother-in-law wasn't turning into one of the peaceniks. "What are you doing here? What about school?"

Ned shrugged and gave him a fine enigmatic smile. "I got kicked out."

"How come?"

Ned stood on one hip, looking at the floor and lazily scratching the back of his neck. "Well, I could tell you a lot of stories but the truth is I got caught balling the wife of the head of the history department in a broom closet and all hell broke loose and when it was all over it was suggested that maybe I should pursue my education elsewhere."

Don laughed. "No? Really? Caught in a broom closet!"

Ned looked rueful. "Ever try to put your pants on while you're running down a hall stark naked with an irate husband swinging at you and his wife screaming bloody murder up and down the hall?"

They laughed together and Don held a shushing finger to his lips, pointing to the sleeping form of Kathy on the couch. Briefly, he explained what had happened and they carried Ned's suitcase and sleeping bag into the bedroom. Don got drinks and closed the bedroom door. He was delighted to see Ned and, as they sat and drank and joked, it reminded him of good times in Saigon, nights when they stayed up and drank. He liked Ned, liked his honesty and, as they talked, he found he could tell him things about the war that he had kept locked up inside of him. Ned was a good listener and said, "Yeah, I've been thinking about upping. Hell, I'm bored. I'd like to see a little of that life over there. I mean, that's where the action is. It's all that basic bullshit, all that spit and polish you go through, that stops me."

"Yeah, it's a drag. Sometimes I think of re-upping. Most of the time, I don't know what the hell I want."

They sat, relaxed, drinking. "Yeah, I know the feeling. Hey, how was the poontang over there. Fill me in, man."

They talked on, their voices low and confidential, drinking, laughing together over sexual adventures. Ned listened closely, his eyes glinting like some predatory bird sizing up a potential meal.

Finally, he leaned forward, nudging Don's knees. "Listen, last time I was here, I got to know a chick. Her name is Tina O'Toole. Wild? Out of sight. A real far out broad for real."

"What's she like?" Don asked, feeling the scotch and a certain man-to-man smuttiness.

"She's a topless, bottomless, double-clutching, breech-loading, high-stepping, gear-shifting, air-cooled, free-wheeling wild dancer. Didn't Kathy tell you about it?"

Don shook his head and tried to keep calm. "No, she never mentioned it." Perhaps he was going to find out some of what was bothering her.

Ned shrugged and nodded understandingly. "I took her to one of those topless-bottomless places. She had never been. The chick there, Tina, turned me on and so I met her."

"Ah," Don said, holding up a finger. "That's what's bothering her. She told me you were kind of wild when you were here."

"Wild?" Ned looked like he was posing

for a picture as the innocent angel. "Wild? Me?" Then his lips spread in that crooked insinuating smile and Don slapped him on the knee.

"Probably the whole thing upset her. I mean, the place and you, her brother, making out with a dancer. You know how she is."

"Yeah," Ned grinned. "Only it didn't upset her and I didn't make out with Tina until later. I told Kathy I was going back to school and went back down and shacked up with Tina for two long gruelling days. I tell you, she is out of sight. No bull, just a straight come-on and hop right into bed."

"No kidding?"

"An inexhaustible fucking machine."

"No kidding?"

"Wake up in the middle of the night with her going down on me. Listen, I'm going to see her for sure this trip. Like to meet her?"

Flattered, Don laughed and said, "Why not? Always wanted to meet a fucking machine."

"Great!" Ned said enthusiastically. "Tell you what. Tomorrow night we'll all go down to the club and you can catch her act."

"She really strip? All the way?"

"All the way and believe me, what you'll see is nothing compared to what she does in a bedroom."

"Too much, huh?" Don asked, his mouth

a little open, his cock beginning to jerk and swell in his pyjamas.

"Listen, I'll tell you a little of what she does. Ever heard of using whipped cream? Puts it all over your cock then eats it off."

"Really?"

Ned grinned sardonically. "And that's just for openers. Like she says: If you cum on that, it don't count."

The two laughed together, Don amazed by Ned's outlook and excited by the prospect of meeting such a girl as Tina. Ned went on regaling him with her lewd and bizarre conduct. He described her body in detail and topped it all with, "And guess what? She's only just turned seventeen. Honest! She's so built, she looks far older. Phony I.D. allows her to work in a nightclub. We'll all go down to see her tomorrow night. What say?"

Don was only too eager to agree when he remembered Kathy. "No good. Doctor says she's got to stay off her feet for a few days."

Ned looked concerned and nodded. "Tell you what. Why don't I bring her up here after her show? Man, that would be a gas. Kathy will get tired and go to bed and I'm sure I can talk Tina into a private show."

Don's cock gave a leap. "It would be wild," he said, dubious that such a thing should ever happen.

Ned reached and punched him on the

shoulder. "Like old times in Vietnam, I bet. Tell me about over there. Ever smoke any of that Vietnam grass?"

And there the discussion took a new turn with Ned admitting and producing some grass and Don tiptoeing to the door to check on Kathy before lighting up and smoking and relaxing into a rambling euphoria where he talked of the war and, eventually, his buddy. They ended the talk with both silent and drugged. Ned stirred himself, unrolled his sleeping bag and fell asleep on the floor. Don crawled into bed thinking of all the kids who had been wounded and killed. Thinking of the body of his roommate and best buddy Greg when he was asked to identify it.

When you can go like that, he thought, quick and without warning, when you can go for no good reason at all, what the hell difference does anything make? Live it up.

He rolled over on his face and fell asleep, determined he would somehow have the dancer, Tina, over to their house that night.

Chapter 6

Kathy woke early, looking around, locating herself and sitting up. She felt sleepy still, but rested. She put some weight on her feet and found she could hobble to the bedroom. The shock of seeing Ned on the floor and the empty glasses and bottle made her catch her breath. She retreated from the room hastily, shutting the door and retreating to the couch. She sat, trying to think of what to do. With an impulse, she thought of leaving the apartment, going away until he had left. Yet, where could she go? All her clothes were in the bedroom.

She sat, resigned, that strange sad look coming into her eyes again. With a deep sigh, she got to her feet and made her way to the kitchen where she started preparing breakfast. Both of her men would be hungry.

It was Ned who awoke first, rubbing his face then listening. Noises coming from the kitchen, small early morning cup-and-saucer noises. He got up noiselessly, put on his pants and crept to the kitchen. Kathy was standing with her back to the door when he entered.

He hadn't made a sound yet he saw her back stiffen. She felt him behind her. She turned slowly, looking at him with large grave eyes.

He took her in quickly. She had changed physically. Something different in her face. Maybe it was self-pity. Whatever it was, it was a sign to Ned. She still wasn't broken. She was still full of pretence, she was still a "good girl." She still wasn't what he called, "Liberated." She still felt guilt and felt there was a "normal" way to behave in bed.

It was with a thin lipped grin that, he crossed the room in his bare feet, thinking: I'll take care of her.

He took her in his arms and kissed her on the mouth, running his tongue in and out as one hand closed over her buttocks. "Hiya, Babe," he whispered, pulling his mouth away. "I'm back."

Kathy was fighting him with all her strength, glancing over his shoulder toward the bedroom. "Ned!" she hissed, hitting his bare chest with her fists. "Don is in there! Stop it!"

For an answer, Ned thrust his hips forward and rubbed his groin against hers. Under his pants, he was as naked as she was under her housecoat. "Been a long time, Babe. I want to fuck that little million volt pussy of yours again."

"Stop that talk! You're insane!" she

whispered fiercely, fighting to pull away but feeling her strength and resolution ebbing fast. She fought against a animal desire to throw open her housecoat and let him fuck her right on the kitchen floor with her husband, Don, joining in. Let him watch her brother fucking her, let the two of them do anything they wanted to her! "Oh, Ned," she moaned, trying feebly to pull away. "Why did you have to come back? " she wailed, her voice rising slightly.

Ned let go of her, looked over his shoulder and walked to the table and slid on a chair. "How about some black coffee?" he asked in a cheery voice.

His luck or intuition held. Don was up and coming out, yawning and stretching. "Well, he's here. Hey, what are you doing on your feet?" he asked, taking Kathy in his arms and kissing her.

A horny thrill ran through her. She felt her cunt moist and itching with desire between her thighs as she looked at Ned grinning at her with that wild look on his face. No matter what else she felt, it was exciting, being caressed by two different men one right after the other.

"Well, there he is. Does he look all right? Only thing wrong with him is a broom closet."

"What?" Kathy asked and the two men

laughed.

She was led back to the couch and, while they both made breakfast and kidded back and forth in the kitchen, she tried hard to compose herself and make light banter back. She learned that Ned had left school by Popular request and her mind imagined what had happened in the closet and she insanely wished that it had been her, that they had thrown the door open and caught them fucking and they had gone on, right in front of them.

She jerked herself back to reality with the silent warning that such thoughts were bad and the dreaded admittance that she thought of them – sex fantasies – increasingly. She sat on the couch and watched her brother and husband with increasing disbelief. They got along so well together and Ned was so charming and full of locker room camaraderie with Don. At times, she sat stunned by the secrets she held when she watched Ned's seemingly innocent yet brazen behavior. His audacity was unbelievable! They sat in the living room, and the late afternoon sun slanted long into the room. Don had mixed a batch of martinis while Ned was playing a Rolling Stones album on the stereo he had rushed out to purchase, Don driving him to the nearest record store, and was now enthusiastically trying to get Kathy and Don to like the music.

Don was tolerant and unimpressed. They sat sipping their drinks until Ned suddenly, again, unpredictably, leaping to his feet and snapping the stereo off. He looked down at Don with a smile twitching his lips. Then he turned and stared seriously at Kathy on the couch. He turned back to Don, his face set and serious. "I've got something to tell you. Something I wanted to tell you last night."

His manner, his tone of voice made Don sit up. "Well, what?"

Again Ned swung around to face Kathy on the couch. It seemed her face was drained of all colour and the knuckles of her hand tightened, growing white, around the glass she held. She didn't breathe or blink. She couldn't. She was frozen with fear.

Ned looked back at Don. "Kathy and I have a secret," he said, his voice low and each word loud and clear.

Don stiffened, not sure of what he was going to hear; not sure that he wanted to hear it. "Okay," he said gravely, "Let's hear it."

Ned looked hard at Don then Kathy for a moment and Kathy felt as if she were on the verge of screaming, a scream she wouldn't be able to stop.

"Well, when I was here before, when you were away, we... no, it was me. I made Kathy do something."

Don licked his lips and nodded. It was coming, the whole sordid mess, he thought. His eyes flicked at Kathy who was sitting like a marble statue, her eyes riveted on her brother. "What," Don asked in a low voice, "Did you make Kathy do?"

Ned held a palm out, "Well, actually I talked her into it. Listen, it's all my fault and I take the blame. It was my idea and..."

"Get to it!" Don said, his face hard.

"Well," Ned suddenly looked like a charming boy, abashed at what he had done. "I talked her into smoking some grass."

The three of them seemed caught in a frozen tableau for an eternity of seconds before Don took on a look of amusement and threw back his head and laughed and Kathy seemed to grow smaller and sag back in relief on the couch, a silly dazed smile on her lips while Ned kicked his toe into the carpet, winked at Kathy then turned a lamb-like face to Don. "Like I said, it's all my fault."

"That's it!" Don said, pointing at his wife who tried to laugh back. "That's what's been bugging you! Even after I told you I had smoked it!" He was up, grinning, going to his wife and kissing her on the mouth. "You were worried! How did you feel, like some dope fiend?" he asked.

Kathy hugged him, thankful her brother hadn't just come out and told all the truth. She wasn't completely sure that he wouldn't just for the hell of it, come right out and say it.

Her relief was by no means entirely artificial and she seized the opportunity to feel closer to her husband. He had her in his arms and she was looking over his shoulder at her brother standing slouched in the middle of the room, grinning at her, immensely pleased with himself.

Don seemed elated that his doubts were so easily assuaged; he drank and laughed and got up, slapping Ned on the shoulder. "You son-of-a-gun! I might have known!" He was suddenly full of questions and plans. He discovered that Ned could get some. With a broad wink that Kathy couldn't see, he asked Ned. "How long will it take?"

"Well, it depends. I could make a phone call."

It was agreed and Ned went into the bedroom to make the call. Kathy motioned to Don to come close to her so that Ned wouldn't hear. "Don, I don't want to take any."

"Ah, come on, it's all right."

"I mean it. I don't like what... I just don't like it."

Don was too elated to really listen. He drained his glass and poured himself a generous amount of straight scotch. He raised his glass in a mock toast. "Don't be a prude. Listen, I tell you it's all right. Little grass won't hurt a thing."

Kathy stared up at her husband filled with a dread of what was coming. He was standing in front of her, drinking, gulping. She knew his pattern. If he kept on like this, he would soon be drunk. A premonition, a sudden flashing sense of what was going to happen: a presage of doom. Don drunk, smoking marijuana and Ned urging him on, biding his time like some smiling predatory animal. Ned sitting in the background until Don is too drunk and too drugged and passes out. Then?

"Don, please don't drink too much," she said in a soft, plaintive voice.

"'S'allright. Look, honey, we used to drink night n'day over there," he said with an extravagant wave of his arm. "Fly one of them choppers smashed, can do anything."

Ned came into the room, grinning shyly at Kathy then looking self-conscious in front of Don. "Look, remember that girl Tina I told you about last night? Well, she's got some and she's got the night off. How about if I ask her over?"

"Sure! Why not? S'allright, honey? Sure it is! What the hell!"

Ned left, grinning at Kathy, borrowing the car keys to go pick Tina up. Kathy was left sitting on the couch, her face a mask. Calmly, she said, "Don, you're mixing scotch with martinis. Do you think that's a good idea?"

Don, sitting across the room slumped in a chair, made a face. "Ah, come on," he said, his lips twisting, "You're not going to be a nagging wife are you?"

She looked down at the empty drink in her hands. "No," she answered in a small voice.

"Better not," he muttered, staring into his glass. "I didn't come home to listen to somebody bitch me 'cause I felt like having a drink or two." His voice and manner were sullen and he stared down at his drink before suddenly gulping it down and getting unsteadily to his feet and heading for the kitchen to pour himself another drink.

An anger blazed in Kathy. If her own husband didn't care, why should she? She held her drink aloft. "If there are any more martinis, I'd like another."

"Thatta girl," he said, grinning at her and taking her glass. "Gonna be an interesting night."

"And how," she answered with a bitter sarcasm in her voice that seemed to go right over Don's head, thanks to his numbing drinks.

She got Don to help her to the bedroom where she checked her a appearance and brushed her hair then got into bed. She was working on her third martini when the doorbell rang.

With the bedroom door open, she could see a portion of the living room. Kathy's heart stopped when she saw who Ned's girl friend was: it was the dancer they had seen together what seemed so very long ago! Good grief! Ned was even more diabolical than she had given him credit for.

The girl stood in the middle of the room, wearing an Indian headband and a fringed buckskin miniskirt. Her bare thighs and legs were tanned. She was tall, well-shaped with dark almond eyes that flashed suggestively as she looked around the apartment and into the bedroom where she saw Kathy sitting erect in bed. A slow lascivious smile spread over her thick shapely lips, as she shifted her weight, thrusting out one hip and putting a hand on it. She lowered her head, her smile all-knowing. "Hi," she said in a throaty voice, "I'm Tina."

Kathy closed her eyes and nodded. Women have a way of understanding each other far better than men do. A look, a word, a gesture, an intonation, can say so much. Men tend to make little of such scenes, putting it down as jealousy, as petty vain rivalry. Women know better: Tina had just told Kathy that she knew all about her and Kathy had accepted and silently pleaded for mercy.

They all came pouring into the bedroom with introductions and explanations all around about Kathy's accident. They sat on chairs with Tina sitting on the edge of the bed with a newly poured drink in her hand, smiling down at Kathy. "Your brother didn't do you justice."

"Oh?" Kathy looked at Ned who was busy stuffing a long pipe with a thick gummy substance.

"You're much more beautiful than he said," Tina said in a cool way.

Kathy tried to wince out a smile. "Why... thank you."

"Damn right," Don said, looking at Tina. "Hey!" he said loudly, "What is that, Ned?" he asked, turning to watch Ned.

"Something better. Hash. Seems Tina had some and wanted to donate it."

Don turned and grinned at Tina again, his eyes taking in her smooth bare thighs and her heavy pointed breasts under her dress. Damn, he thought, I don't think she's wearing a bra.

Kathy knew she wasn't. Having her sitting there, shifting her weight, she could gee her breasts move freely under the buckskin. She had seen Tina naked and knew how high-riding her breasts naturally were.

"Say, are you really Indian?" Don asked, obviously fascinated by her exotic beauty and excited by what Ned had told him about her. He crossed his legs and sipped at his drink, feeling his cock growing thick between his thighs. "I mean, do you have Indian blood somewhere in the family?"

Tina gave him a dazzling seductive smile. "Yes, my mother was a full-blooded Cherokee, my father was a redheaded Scottish policeman in Kiowa, Kansas. I guess I'm what they call a half- breed."

Don laughed and patted her on the shoulder. "What a combination. Couldn't be better."

"For what?" Tina asked in a low seductive voice, flirting with him over the edge of her drink.

Don's face coloured and he drank from his glass before answering, "Oh, well... anything, I guess."

Ned interrupted with the pipe. He lit it expertly and quickly handed it to Don who puffed and rose to sit on the bed next to Tina. He exhaled and handed the pipe to Tina. "Pass the peace pipe, huh?"

Again, Tina smiled at him with an inviting look. "Depends on what you mean by 'peace'," she said, accenting the word.

Ned and Don laughed as Tina took the pipe into her mouth slowly, closing her lips over the stem with a loving, "Mmmm."

They passed the pipe around, crowding closer on the bed. Kathy looked to see their smiling faces watching her as she puffed on the pipe. The hashish was having an effect and she felt like she was on a celestial elevator, zooming up so fast she felt as if she had left her body and reason far down below. This, she thought, is what they must mean by getting 'high.'

The room was suddenly very quiet and thick with a pungent sweet smoke and everything seemed to be moving in ultra slow motion. It seemed to Kathy she had accepted, puffed on and passed the hashish pipe hundreds of times, that they would never smoke it all. She stared absently at the faces around her. Don had taken on a glazed look and might be some child watching a movie or TV. He didn't seem conscious of anyone around him until he started, rubbed his face and said, "Wow!" in a soft voice and look at Tina with his eye slitting and growing hungry.

Ned seemed bemused, his fist propping up his chin as he watched Don and Tina, ignoring Kathy. Tina straightened her shoulders, thrusting her breasts forward toward Don so that her nipples pressed against the soft tawny buckskin. Her dark Indian eyes slid slowly to Kathy and wandered over her body, taking in all she could see.

Ned slapped his hands on his knees and said, "Let's have a little music and some more to drink."

Don tore his eyes from Tina and said, "Hey, that's a great idea." He got to his feet and went into the living room after collecting all the glasses. Tina, with a lazy smile, said, "Let me help you."

Kathy was left looking at Ned who was staring off into space, that wolf-like smile on his face again. "Ned, don't, please don't. In God's name, don't."

He turned innocent eyes to her. "Don't what?" he asked then chuckled to himself and got to his feet and walked to the door, his hand on the knob. Looking over his shoulder, he gave a cruel wink. "You gotta rest. I'll tell Don. And," he whispered, closing the door, "I'll be back."

The door closed slowly and firmly and Kathy leaned back on the pillows and closed her eyes. There seemed nothing she could do to stop what was happening. Nothing, in her drugged state, she wanted to do. With an anguished thought, she realized that there really was nothing she wanted to do. She drained her glass and wished for sleep.

Tina followed Don to the kitchen, her hips swaying back and forth. She stood watching him mixing the drinks, her hands on her hips, her pelvis thrust out. Don gave her a flirting glance. What the hell, he thought, no harm done and it's not like I'm an old man yet. "Ned says you're a dancer."

Tina, smiling, her chin tucked in so that she looked at him seductively, said, "That's right. Come watch me some time."

"I'd like to," he said, handing her a drink. "Do you like it?"

"Dancing? Or do you really mean do I like dancing in front of men naked? The answer to both questions is… yes." Again she smiled seductively at him over the rim of her glass, showing her fine white teeth.

Don looked at her, finding it impossible to believe she was so young. Her face was unlined and looked young but her body was so fully and wildly developed. From the living room came music from the stereo. Ned had selected some quite cool jazz And Tina began to swing her hips in a slow brazen manner. "I just hear music and then I gotta move."

Don leaned drunkenly against the kitchen table and watched her begin to dance, her feet staying in place, only her body moving, undulating, her hips suddenly twitching out in time to the music. Her arms above her head, she danced into the living room with Don lurching after her. He saw her fall into Ned's arms and kiss him passionately on the mouth while her hips ground into his crotch and Don could see her firm young buttocks tense and bunch under her miniskirt. "Hey," he said, waving his glass, "Let's have a party."

Ned tore himself free to gasp, "Man, it

looks like we are!"

"No!" Don said, falling into a chair and spilling some of his drink. "I mean a real party with entertainment." He leered at Tina who had turned to look at him. She danced slowly and sensuously toward him, halting right in front of him, her arms slowly raising to cup her breasts and thrust them at his face while her hips did a slow wicked bump and grind.

"Look, don't get this chick started. I'm warning you, Don," Ned said. Then, "Hey, where's my drink?"

"'Sin the kitchen," Don said, slurring his words and never taking his eyes off Tina's wiggling body. "and take your ole sweet time gettin' it."

Ned gave him a comradely wink and said, "Think I'll take a drink in to Kathy and keep my little sister company for awhile."

He disappeared into the kitchen while Tina continued dancing, whirling around the room, her eyes half closed. Ned came back into the room with two drinks in his hands and a child-like foolish grin on his face. "I'm so stoned I don't know what I'm doing. You okay?" he asked Don.

Don nodded absently, still watching Tina dance. Ned noted with satisfaction that his eyes were glazed and he was having trouble focusing them. Tina would keep him busy. He turned the door knob to the bedroom with his fingers and shoved the door open with his elbow. This, he told himself, was going to be some night. Tina working on Don while he taught his prissy married sister a lesson. And Tina knowing all about it!

Don tore his eyes from Tina long enough to see Ned kicking the door shut with his heel. Tina stopped dancing and picked up her glass, sipping from it as she walked toward him. "Hey, Tina," he said, "Don't stop. You're pretty good."

Tina gave a laugh. "I'd better or I'll start getting rough and raunchy." She drank and raised her glass as a toast. "The only way I know how to dance."

Don drained his glass and said, "I'll drink to that. I mean, I'd really like to see you dance." He struggled up out of his chair to get still another drink. Tina pushed him back in his seat and said, "Let me do that. " He sat back, dazed, watching her firm young buttocks switch back and forth as she sauntered into the kitchen. While she was gone, he tried to clear his head, rubbing his eyes. Gotta think clear, he told himself.

He looked up to see Tina standing in front of him with two fresh drinks in her hand, smiling down at him. Jesus, he thought, how long has she been standing there? He took the drink with a vague. smile. His brain seemed fogged and he couldn't think straight. All he could think about was Tina's body and her whipped cream trick. But his wife was in the next room with his brother- in-law! He had better be careful, he thought.

Tina suddenly bent over him and kissed him on the mouth, the tip of her hot wet tongue darting into his mouth and sending shudders down into his groin that caused his cock to leap in lewd excitement. "You're nice," she whispered in his ear.

His free hand touched her hip and he felt her naked flesh under the sensuous deerskin. "You're okay," he whispered.

Her face was close to his, her eyes large, dark, and burning, as she whispered, "Want me to dance for you?"

His mind raced, drunken, drugged and ramming, horny, wild, mad! Why not, he thought, exulting drunkenly, after all, it was Ned who brought her! "Yeah," he breathed, "Go ahead!"

He sat, his cock throbbing, caught in his pants, swelling painfully and he tried to rearrange his legs, self-conscious now, crossing them, so it wouldn't show.

Tina put her glass down and stepped back from him, moving slowly, her eyes closed, a smile on her face, her hips swaying as she lifted her arms and pulled the miniskirt up over her head. Don sat, his face impacted, his breath shallow as he watched the limp buckskin being pulled up her tanned thighs. Up, up, higher and higher until her face was covered and she was naked from the waist down. He looked at her broad swaying hips and her long thighs with his eyes drawn to her sparse young wedge of curling pubic hair. She turned, standing on tiptoe and pulled the dress free over her head and flung it on the floor.

She stood with her back to him, naked gave for sandals and her Indian headband. Lewdly, moving in pulsating time to the music, she leaned forward and thrust her naked round buttocks at him and Don gazed open mouthed as he saw her tight vagina trapped between her strong thighs with its vaginal lips firm and covered with dark downy pubic hair. In time to the music, she turned, her arms widespread, her legs apart, her knees bent. Slowly, as he watched, she began moving her hips and cunt as if she had the tip of a cock right in front of her thighs and was trying to rub against it. She threw back her head, her eyes closed, her mouth open and her pelvis rolled forward and she let out a little delighted moan and her body shuddered as if an invisible cock had been shoved in her and she began an imaginary fucking right in front of Don who dropped his drink on the rug and ignored it as he lurched to his feet, breathing heavily.

Tina was on him like a cat, a cat on heat, twining her lithe arms tight around him, her open mouth locked to his as his tongue darted in and out while one of her long tanned dancer's legs slipped around behind him and pulled his groin close to hers. He felt his ramrod cock against her naked belly and he fought to get away from her, catch his breath. "No! " he breathed. "My wife and... Ned," he said, pointing.

Tina's face was intense. "So what? Now or never for me and you. Come on, what have you got to lose?"

"Everything!"

"Coward!" she said, voice harsh with contempt, almost spitting the words.

A wild idea entered his mind. Ned had done it in a closet! Why not top him? Kathy couldn't walk and he could, would, no – had to, think of something. More than anything, he wanted to fuck this wild, amoral half-breed bitch! He lurched into the kitchen and opened the closet. It was big enough – with just a single suitcase on the floor which he shoved aside with his foot. Tina was right behind him, pushing him into the tight space. They closed the door behind them. He turned to find her hot naked body right against his. Her hands guided his up until he touched her breasts and he felt them soft and heavy in his hands and his fingers pinched her nipples and he felt them grow hard and pointed as he watched her tongue slowly lick her lips. He felt her hand unzipping his pants and he closed his eyes and kissed her as he felt her groping fingers pulling his hard cock out. Her hands closed over it, squeezing it and pulling back the foreskin and slowly and surely stroking back and forth as her tongue darted in and out of his mouth in time to the strokes.

He felt dizzy with passion and a violent urge welled up in him. He wanted to fuck the teasing little bitch with all his might, fuck her until she begged for mercy. His whole body was tense as he felt her knees bending, their mouths wetly parting as she slid down to her knees, her hands holding onto his hard cock. Drunkenly, he put his arms out for support, finding the walls in the semi-darkness and standing balanced while looking down, he could see the top of her head and those big rounded breasts below. She was on her knees and straightening her back again, thrusting her breasts upward and outward and placing his prick, its foreskin rolled all the way back to reveal its pinkish-mauve mushroom head, between her breasts, wedging it into the deep cleavage then using her hands to cup her breasts close together so that his cock was surrounded and held in place by the hot soft flesh of her breasts with only the thick rampant head visible.

She bent her head to look down at it and, with an electric thrill searing through him, he felt her wet hot tongue flick across it, teasing the glans on the very end. He saw her look up and smile and smack her lips, greedily tasting the drop of clear pre-cum she had urged from him. Her head swooped again and he felt the flat of her tongue lick all over his prick and he thrust his hips forward just as her incredibly soft and wet lips closed over the head and she sucked while her tongue twirled downward and his head fell back limply as he moaned aloud.

The whole shaft of his prick felt encased in warm soft moving flesh while the head felt her hot mouth sucking on it with the tongue tormenting it into a swelling that hurt him. He wanted her, he wanted to fuck her silly. He'd show her what a real fuck was like. Roughly, he pushed her away, the back of her head bumping against the closet door, knocking it open, allowing her to sprawl out on the kitchen floor, her breasts quivering like jello, her long nude body flowing out, her legs spread wide so that he looked down and saw the glistening red slit of her cunt.

With a hoarse cry, he fell from the closet, landing on top of her. His cock pushed, felt her vaginal lubricated lips rubbing against

the thick head of his cock. Thrusting with his hips, he felt her cunt spreading in a slow extraordinarily sensual way. He pushed hard and he felt it sink home, into the hot depths of her cunt. Her long legs wrapped around his buttocks and pulled him in while her hips writhed up so that he felt his cock travel still further, as deep as it could go.

They exploded in a frenzy of movement. Don, jaw clenched, fucked her with all his might, with a wild insane abandon. Tina held him tight, her hips moving as fast as she could while she moaned and her head thrashed back and forth. He was fucking her so hard her hips and buttocks came clear of the floor and then were sent crashing, thumping down again as he used all his strength to ram his prick home in her. In front of him he could just dimly see her open mouth with her eyes rolling in her head as she thrashed around, writhing under him. He was fucking her across the floor, digging in with his knees on the rug and slamming down on her so that she saw stars. They were fucking their way into the middle of the room so that there was no place to hide or no possible explanation to make if Ned should open the door. And Don didn't care. His mouth twisted open as be felt the mighty hurricane rush of an orgasm sweep through him and funnel out his prick and explode wetly inside of the girl and he bit her hard on the shoulder to keep from shouting.

His face twisting in a wild drunken, drugged exultation, he rolled off her and flopped on his back, gasping for breath. Tina was on top of him immediately, kissing him. He pushed her off and got to his hands and knees and started to crawl from the kitchen, Tina after him. She was excited, sexually voracious, and needed to be satisfied. She pawed at him on the kitchen floor as he fought to catch his breath. "Come on " she gasped.

"No." He shook his head, exhausted, looking down at his cock. It was still hard even though white hot sperm, his own cum, was still dripping from it. "Too dangerous," he gasped, shaking his head. "That was crazy. They must have heard."

"No, no, they didn't!" Tina said in a low voice. "Don't worry, it's all right. Come on, I'm horny and hot!"

Don held her by the shoulders. "They must have heard."

"No, no!" Tina insisted, her eyes glinting as she crawled on top of him, thrusting one of her breasts in his face.

"*It doesn't matter!*"

Her words froze him. How could she know it didn't matter unless – unless she knew something! He grabbed her by the shoulders, full of a sudden rage. Tina recoiled and found herself helpless in his iron grip. "What do you mean?"

"Nothing. I meant I want to cum too!"

"What do you mean, it doesn't matter?" he asked, his voice hard.

"I meant it doesn't matter if they catch us," she said in a lame voice, her face telling him she was lying.

His drugged and drunken state was like storm clouds dark, thick, and heavy in his mind and her words were like a parting of the clouds and a flash of lucid lightening in his brain. "What's going on here? I mean, what's really going on here?"

He suspected a monstrous evil sick trick was being played on him. With a madman's strength, he whirled Tina around and clapped a hand over her mouth. He grated into her ear, "You be quiet or you'll be sorry!" With a controlled fury, he forced her to her feet and dragged her, naked, his prick still hanging out of his pants, back into the living room and toward the bedroom door.

When they got near the door Tina's leg lashed out, trying to kick it. Don hadn't expected that and his drunken and drugged nerves reacted too late. He pulled her away as the door flew open and bounced away from the wall.

The scene that greeted them turned both of them to marble. Don couldn't move or speak or even think. Slowly, unconsciously, he let go of Tina. He stood, looking into his own bedroom, at his own bed, at his wife and her brother on the bed, naked.

Ned was lying on his back, his legs spread wide and Kathy, his wife, was on top of him, her legs to either side of his waist, on her knees. And, as he watched in stupid amazement, he saw her naked buttocks exposed to his view, her anus puckered and tight and below, her soft, hair fringed cunt was wet and split wide. It was stretched as far as it could go and as he watched her hips move obscenely up and down her brother's huge thick prick, as he watched its glistening shaft disappear into her cunt, folding the tight vaginal lips in, then saw her lift her body, saw the juicy pink walls of her cunt rolling out, seeming to cling to the fat length of the slippery cock with all their might, he knew; he knew that what was happening was worse than any expectations. He was being cuckolded by his very own brother-in-law, he was witnessing the worst sort of incest – the sort that involved those close to him!

His mind exploded as they fucked on, oblivious of him, Ned's hands massaging Kathy's lovely breasts in a lewd and exciting rhythm. With a roar, he hit out at Tina with the back of his hand, sending her flying. He rushed into the room and grabbed his wife

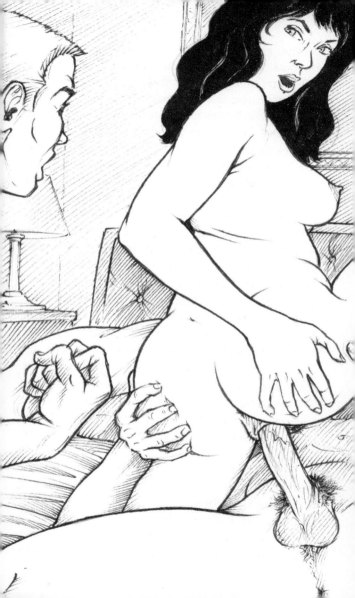

by the shoulders and sent her crashing off the bed. Ned was leaping up just in time to dodge a fist square in the face. It hit him a glancing blow. He fell backward and off the bed, his mind reeling. Don was on top of him, punching and slapping at him ineffectually as he sobbed and screamed out his rage and hate. With a snarl, he whirled and tried to slap his wife's but his aim was poor and Kathy was ready to duck him.

He leaped to his feet, his fists ready. Brother and sister cowered on the floor, looking up at him. Blood trickled from a small abrasion on Ned's cheek where Don's ring had cut him.

"Scum!" he spat at them, "Rotten perverted scum! So that was it! Well, I'm through, you hear?" With an insane strength, he picked Ned up. Ned held his hands up. With a cold calculation, he threw him down again then whirled on his wife, seizing her by her hair and lifting her to her feet. "And you, you perverted bitch!" he growled.

"I couldn't help it! I tried to tell you!" she wailed.

With a look of contempt twisting his face, he shoved her from him. "I'll be back tomorrow to get my things and deal with you!" He stood in the middle of the room, putting his penis back into his pants and shaking with rage. "When I come back, I don't want to see your sick face!" he said, turning to Ned who was on the floor, nursing his cut. "Where are the car keys?"

Ned, still in a state that bordered somewhere between shock and stoned out of his mind, motioned to the night table by the bed. Don scooped them up and stalked from the room. In the living room, Tina was on the couch, her dress held in front of her body. He glared at her with tight lips. She threw a sullen look back at him, as if to say 'Why did you have to go and spoil it all?' which made him no less angry.

They all had been in on it and he would make them pay, he would make them wish they had never tried to make a fool of him. He stepped out of the little apartment and slammed the door shut with all his might, the sound booming and echoing down the hall.

Chapter 7

Kathy lay naked on the floor, hearing the sound of the door slamming, knowing that Don never slammed a door, knowing that it was a doomsday bell, tolling in her brain. It seemed as if the sound went on and on, growing louder. The whole building, the block, the city, the whole world would know of her incestuous behaviour. Of course they would, her paranoid mind told her. She was the town slut, after all, the incestuous whore who liked to fuck her brother.

When Ned had come into her room bearing drinks, she knew what was going to happen. He had undressed in front of her until he stood naked with his huge cock held in one hand, a drink in the other. Even before he spoke, she began taking off her clothes with trembling fingers, a desperate sexual itch growing ever hotter in her loins. "Don't worry, Tina's going to keep him very, very busy," Ned grinned with a jerk of his head toward the door. She was helpless, as she lay naked, her legs spread obediently apart, while he loomed over her.

Now that Don had discovered everything, an odd relief mingled with her agony. At least it was all out in the open now. Whatever Don decided to do, she deserved it. She put her head in her hands and sobbed.

Ned was up on his feet, his fists clenched, glaring out of the bedroom, "That chintzy coward! See him run! Lucky for him I got some self-control. I'd like him to come back here so I can punch him one in the mouth!"

Tina appeared in the doorway, her face calm, composed, and disgusted. She leaned against the doorjamb, naked, but holding her dress over one arm and regarded Ned with a cool unblinking gaze. "Okay, you macho man, you can cut it out now, 'coz nobody's fuckin' listening, are they?"

Ned looked over her shoulder at the empty living room, his eyes narrowing. "Ha! I just wish he would come back so I could work him over!"

Tina had seen and heard scenes like this before. In her world anything went, and that meant people with hurt feelings. She glanced at Kathy huddled on the floor then looked back at Ned. "This is all just a big drag, you know."

"Huh? " He looked at her with uncomprehending eyes.

"Big time, you said. Told me it would be really far out. Yeah – you balling your sister – and a real good time for me. Told me I'd plead for it to stop." She nodded towards Kathy whose shoulders still heaved with heartbreaking sobs. "Look where it's really at, you dumb jerk – you've just ruined your sister's fuckin' life!"

"Oh yeah?" he growled, looking around at his sister. That mad governing drive that possessed him, that wild reckless compulsion that had forced countless situations and gotten him into all kinds of trouble, that black and evil spirit that engulfed his soul and would eventually lead to his doom raged up in him. No one, least of all a woman, was going to put him down. No matter what the cost, he would emerge triumphant. "Oh yeah?" he repeated in a challenging voice. "Okay," he said, shoving his face into Tina's. "You wanted action, you're going to get it! Let's see just what kind of a swinger you are!"

He leaped across the room and picked Kathy up by her wrists. "Shut up! Just shut up and listen to me!" he hissed at her. "Do as I say!"

Kathy was shocked by his words and looked at him with wide, tear-stained eyes. She looked shockingly vulnerable, but her brother pushed her back on the bed where she fell and closed her eyes, moaning, her legs slightly apart. The silence in the room made her open her eyes and Tina was standing at the foot of the bed, her lewd almond eyes taking in her nude body. "Mmmmmmmm," Tina murmured, letting her dress fall noiselessly to the floor. She looked at Ned standing by the side of the bed with a wicked sidelong look.

Ned wiped his mouth with the back of his hand. "Go on," he said, looking down at Kathy. "Babe, you're going to be hanged for a horse thief, might as well steal the horse."

Kathy put her hands over her eyes. This, after all that had happened, was too much.

"No!"

"*Yes!*" he hissed. "God *damn* you," he raged in a low tight voice. "I want to see you, I want to see you hot and begging for more! I want to see you making love with Tina!"

Kathy pulled her hands away from her eyes, horrified. He couldn't do this to her! Not now! Not ever! He couldn't ask this of her, he couldn't ask her to make lesbian love while he watched, he couldn't, wouldn't, mustn't, ask this depraved act of her. "No!" she whispered, her voice small and trembling. She pulled her legs together and covered up her sex with both hands. Ned was on her in a moment, wedging his hands between her thighs and forcing them apart with his masculine strength.

"Please, no!" Kathy begged, her voice wavering as she saw Tina standing with her legs spread slightly apart, her fingers caressing her cunt as she smiled down at Kathy's protective hands.

"Relax," she whispered, "I can do things to you no man ever can and you'll like them."

Kathy looked at her with pleading eyes as she crawled up on the bed between her legs. Ned relaxed his agonizing grip on her thighs and began prying her hands away, talking all the time in that demanding insistent way of his. "I want you to make love while I watch,

I want to see you get hot and wild and I want to see you cum with your hot little pussy wrapped around another woman's tongue!"

The lewd, insane thought hammered at Kathy's mind as she felt her hands dragged away from her cunt and pinned to the bed above her head. She tried to squeeze her thighs shut but only succeeded in locking them around Tina's waist. "Oh please not that... not that... no!" she breathed as she felt Tina's soft forefinger glide up and down the slit of her cunt. Despite herself, she felt herself responding as the finger lightly played over her clitoris and ran lovingly up and down the lips of her vagina. The teasing aroused her and, as she was opening her mouth to make one last feeble protest, Ned kissed her, running his tongue deep into her sucking mouth.

"Mmmmmm," Tina used the fingers of her other hand to delicately spread Kathy's cunt, looking down as she continued stroking with her forefinger. "She's getting excited."

Ned took his mouth away and clamped it on the nipple of one of her breasts as Tina began sawing a finger in and out of her cunt and Kathy closed her eyes and let her body go as she inwardly gloated at the helplessness and depravity of her position. This would be the most depraved orgasm of all! Her hips began gyrating as Tina let out a

pleased little smile as she twirled her finger in her own passion-moistened cunt while her thumb rubbed Kathy's clitoris and Kathy found herself spreading her legs and rolling her buttocks under, completely exposing the whole of her open cunt to the other girl.

With a wicked and pleased expression, Tina wiggled down on the bed until her shoulders were wedged between Kathy's thighs and her head bent over Kathy's open hot cunt Ned took his mouth from her breast and reaching, propped a pillow under Kathy's head. "I want you to watch her eating your pussy," he said, his voice low and thick with lust.

Kathy looked, excited by her own undulations as she rotated her cunt in front of Tina. Tina cupped her hands under Kathy's buttocks and tilted her hips so that the older woman's hot, wet, fragrant cunt thrust up into the Indian girl's face. And, as Kathy and Ned watched, the tip of Tina's red tongue flicked out and licked the little pink bud of her shamelessly exposed clitoris. A shudder of pure uninhibited pleasure wracked Kathy's body and she moaned, "Oh, God!"

Ned watched as his sister relaxed, her naked body held by Tina and himself in a lewd pose, her legs split obscenely and her hips rotating and undulating obscenely as a look of wicked pleasure twisted her features and she narrowed her eyes to slits and peered down between her jutting breasts and undulating stomach and saw Tina flick her tongue back and forth over her clitoris, exciting her even more. Then, as she gasped and moaned, she saw Tina's head dip a little and she felt the tip of her tongue slide wetly into her cunt.

Her younger brother, beside her, watching with her, shifted his weight and cupped one of her large breasts in his hand and nibbled with his teeth then sucked a nipple. His free hand groped for her hand, found it, grasped it and guided it to her other breast. Kathy, her eyes closed, cupped her own breast willingly, tormenting its stiff, reddened nipple as her hips moved up and down and she felt the girl's tongue licking into her cunt. Nothing mattered any longer but the pleasure that depravity could bring her. Ned, his tongue licking her nipple, crammed a pillow behind her neck, propping her head up against her chest so that she could see Tina's naked body and her bobbing head wedged between her legs. With a moan, she lifted her knees and spread her heels as wide as they could go and felt Tina's hot, ceaselessly wiggling tongue sink deeper and deeper into her lust-maddened cunt. Out of the corner of her eye, she could see Ned licking and sucking at her breast, sending spasms of pure heated pleasure down into her groin where it blended with her ever-growing erotic passion. She closed her eyes in bliss: she would do whatever he wanted, she would even make love to Tina if he wanted her to. Yes, she would like that, maybe... Her own tongue in the sexy Indian girl's pretty pussy... Absently, moaning with a lubricious delight, she again teased the nipple of her other breast, then, knowing why her brother had guided her hand there, she craned her head and tilted the nipple so that she could suck on it, twirl her tongue around it while she closed her eyes and felt tongues caressing and exciting her everywhere.

With a snarl, Ned shattered the even growing rhythm of sucking and licking and Kathy's increasingly abandoned gyrations by pulling away and saying, "I got an idea, I want to see this!"

Tina reluctantly pulled herself free, looking up at Ned with dark burning eyes. Kathy was writhing on the bed, her hands running up and down her body, over her breasts and down over her stomach and hips and sliding over her cunt while her breath came in sharp little hisses.

"Lay down on your back with your head at the foot of the bed," he ordered Tina. She responded with a grin, rolling over on her back with her large tanned breasts rolling. She bent her knees and spread her legs so that Kathy, lying beside her, her head at

Tina's feet, looked between her thighs, at her cunt with its swollen vaginal lips and the glistening slit showing, her excitement.

Ned was off the bed and stalking down to the foot of it, grinning down at Tina who grinned back up and saw his huge thick cock held in his hand. "Get up," he said to Kathy. "Get up on your knees."

Kathy obeyed, rising to her knees with her breasts bunching together temptingly, her hips swaying. Every nerve in her body was screaming for more of the pleasure she had felt and she looked at her brother with that funny helpless look in her eye. "Kneel over her," he commanded in a low voice. "Kneel over her face with your face right over her cunt."

The crude direct obscene command made goosebumps appear on her flesh and she knelt, her knees on either side of Tina's head, felt her fingers tingle up and down the insides of her thighs, and bent forward, putting her weight on her elbows and looking at Tina's hips and her widespread legs and the gently throbbing lips of her begging young cunt.

Her buttocks facing Ned, she moaned long and low when she felt his strong hard hands seize them and order her to spread her legs wide. Then, whimpering, her buttocks twitching and rearing, she felt him spread the lips of her cunt with his thumbs and felt the great thick head of his cock press into the warm wet walls of it. She cried out her lewd delight as she felt her hips being forced apart, felt her cunt stretching painfully as his blood-inflated cock head sunk home with a wet obscene sluicing sound and she knew that Tina was going to see that great cock sawing in and out of her cunt. She was going to watch him fuck her into ecstasy and insensibility.

Her body responded, her hips thrusting backward as Ned thrust in. She wanted to ride the pain of his huge cock, ride it past the stretching and past the blunt savage head banging relentlessly on her cervix and on to the point where she would feel pleasure so intense and thick she would wail with delight and beg for more. Then, a jolt, like high voltage, ran through her body and she stiffened: Tina's tongue was licking her clitoris from below while her brother fucked her from behind!

Her mind went wild and they all began moving in an ever increasing lewd tempo and, closing her eyes, she bent her head and let her tongue lick over the girl's hotly distended cunt. Tina responded by letting her hips move up and down and they were soon undulating together, sweating, in an obscene tempo with Ned gloating over the whole thing, cold-bloodedly pulling his long prick out of his sister's cunt against her moaning protests and bending his knees and guiding his cock into the Indian girl's waiting mouth. A few lubricious strokes and he pulled out and sunk it back into Kathy's waiting cunt.

They heard a noise at the door. Don. He was back in the apartment, framed menacingly in the doorway, staring at the incredible sight of the bodies intertwined on and over the bed.

Don had left the apartment in a fury, running to his car and roaring off. He had driven with a suicidal abandon, screeching around corners until his rational mind took control and he found himself on a freeway and slowed down and allowed himself time to think. What was he going to do? His mind ran amok among several possibilities: tell the police, tell their parents, go back and beat them to within an inch of their lives, never go back, divorce her and, in some way, get even.

More than anything, he wanted to get even. A wild overriding fury possessed him and he realized that he had been shocked cold sober and, while he made his plans, he needed a drink. He pulled off the freeway and found a roadside bar. He sat in the cocktail lounge by himself gulping a double scotch and downing it at once and reordering. He sat over the second scotch, staring off. Yes, he thought once more, more than anything, he wanted to get even. The insane audacity of the two of them! Right in his own house while he was in the next room! What could he do to get even with a stunt like that? A cold cruel grin spread across his face. He tossed his scotch off, ordered another and drank it while paying the bill.

Back in the car, heading back toward town, he felt his head clear and his body calm. He would show them, he would fix them. Above all, he would fix her, his adulterous young whore of a wife.

As he parked the car in front of the apartment, his one worry was that they might have gone. Across the street, he could see old Fuldman looking out of his front window. He grinned coldly. If only the old fart knew...

He tiptoed to his door and listened, holding his breath. No sound. He crouched and squinting one eye, peered through the keyhole. The apartment was silent but the lights were on. Oh yes, they were all still there all right, they were still inside, all in the bedroom. He let himself in slowly, turning the key in the lock with caution, inching the door open silently and just as slowly and quietly closing it and turning the lock shut. No one was going to run out. He tiptoed slowly across the living room, planting each foot carefully and slowly leaning his weight onto it before taking another step.

He held his breath as he neared the door. He heard low muffled sounds and a moan of passion from his wife. The bedroom door was half open and, slipping between the couch and end table, his back against the wall, he looked into the full-length mirror bolted onto the door and saw Kathy sprawled lewd and naked on the bed, on her back with her legs split wide. The Indian girl, naked, the beautiful split of her perfect buttocks facing him, was crouching between Kathy's legs and licking her cunt. A dangerous rage tore at his throat while lust ripped at his groin, swelling his cock as he watched his wife and Tina in a lewd lesbian embrace while Ned, naked, on the bed, was sucking one of Kathy's breasts and, as he watched, his breathing growing excited, he saw her cup and bunch her free breast and suck on the nipple herself! Her lewdness was unbelievable. He watched, bending over the table to get a better view of the obscene tableau going on in the mirror. His mouth was open and sweat was forming on his upper lip as he watched his wife writhe, twist and undulate in a lewd passion he, himself, had never experienced with her.

Suddenly Ned was pulling away and saying something and Don straightened and flattened against the wall, holding his breath, fearful his reflection had been seen in the mirror. He listened, his heart pounding, as he heard Ned giving orders and the sound of bodies shifting on the bed. He waited what seemed an interminable time before leaning out and over the end table again. They had shifted around and he couldn't see all of them so he had to lean further, balancing precariously on one hand. He saw Ned and Kathy's buttocks crouched over the other girl's face. He saw the expression on his wife's face as her brother shoved his big cock in her cunt and he watched, his heart pounding and his cock rock hard in his pants as Ned began enjoying himself, using both of the girls in an obscene way while his wife was so depraved and excited, he saw her lick Tina's cunt while her buttocks twitched and rolled with wild, uninhibited pleasure.

Now, now he'd show them. He twisted and with his free hand, tried to readjust his throbbing prick in his pants and lost his balance and fell with a thump. Instantly, all sound stopped in the bedroom. Don leaped off the end table with a snarl and, moving faster than he thought he could, was standing snarling in the doorway as Ned turned his head to see what made the sound.

For what seemed an eternity of seconds, no one moved or said a word. Ned withdrew his prick from his sister and pointed a finger. "Now wait a minute," he said in a shaky voice, "I... wait a minute... I can..."

"Shut up!" The words hissed through the air and, for once in his life, Ned knew he had better remain silent. Don came slowly into the room, looking at the three of them, menacing, no man to be fooled with, but possessed of an insane coolness and presence of mind. With a jerk of his thumb, he said, "Over there!" to Ned and Ned obeyed, backing away from the bed.

Kathy rolled off of Tina and the two women turned their heads to stare at him with frightened eyes. Another jerk of his thumb told Tina to scamper off the bed and join Ned while Don stood looking down at his wife with cold glittering eyes, a cruel smile playing on his lips. "You like to fuck, huh?" he asked in a low quiet voice, "you like having fun, do you?" he went on as he slowly undressed while Kathy cowered and Tina and Ned held their breath. "You like acting like a whore, is that it? You like feeling like a slut, huh? Oh, really? Turns you on, is that it?" he asked as he flung his underwear to the floor and stood over his wife, stark naked, his cock swollen and blood red, "Well, I'm going to show you what it really feels like. On your belly, *bitch!*" he commanded, the words crackling through the air like a whiplash.

Kathy, although fearful of what would come next, obeyed without a word. She rolled over on the bed, exposing her beautiful, well-rounded buttocks. "Spread your knees and get up on them!" Again, there was a relentless edge to his voice that told her to obey. She got to her knees, her head still down on the mattress and spread her legs so that she was posed obscenely, her cunt wet and split wide.

Don crawled on the bed without even looking at Tina or Ned and spread the cheeks of his young kneeling wife's buttocks and let his thumb rub roughly across her tiny puckered anus. "This," he said with a twisted grin, his voice rough and hoarse, "is what I'm after. The only virgin hole she's got left!"

Kathy gave a sharp cry of pain as he brutally thrust his forefinger into her anus up to the first knuckle joint. She felt it pop lewdly in and held it defensively fast by the rubbery ring of her anus as he wormed it slowly around inside, his fingertip exploring the soft inner walls and teasing at the sensitive flesh.

Then, with a shocking suddenness, his finger was pulled out and her whole body trembled with fear. She knew without a doubt what he was going to do and yet a lewd thrill of humiliation ran through her: She felt she deserved it. This would be the final degradation, the ultimate humiliation: to be sodomized by her outraged husband while her brother and the Indian girl watched.

She whimpered as she felt the head of his cock pushing at the entrance of her anus, sending hot wires of pain shooting electrically through her loins. She lay with her eyes shut tight. It was going to be agony, but she couldn't stop him. *No!* she corrected herself, she didn't *want* to stop him!

She began crying from the pain and pleaded in an incoherent trembling voice, only unintelligible sounds of fear coming from her throat as she felt the iron hard cock pushing inexorably into her rectum as he leaned his weight forward and felt her anal mouth expanding until she felt sure it would split.

"Agggghhhhhhhhha!" she cried as she felt the huge hammering head pop through the tiny puckered entrance. The pain was so great that even Don grimaced as he felt her virginal anal walls snap tight and choking, around his cock. Biting his lips, he pushed further, feeling it sinking deeper and deeper in, the smooth rubbery tightness beginning to be a new lewd thrill.

Kathy felt she would pass out from the pain and she screamed and saw stars dancing in front of her eyes. But her enraged husband only pushed harder, sinking in another cruel lust-hardened inch with the flesh locking tight around his cock as he wormed further and further up and past her tightly constricting anal walls. Slowly, diabolically, he pulled out with her anal flesh clinging obscenely to the cock as though it were glued there. Savagely, then he began thrusting in and out, fucking into and ravaging her rectum insanely as she screamed and cried futilely for mercy.

Ned and the Indian girl were huddled by the wall, watching Don ruthlessly sodomize his wife. They grew excited and caressed one another. Ned, feeling his old manic aggressiveness coming back, put his hands on the girl's shoulders and forced her to her knees where she took his cock in her hands and sucked hungrily on the tip while they watched the scene on the bed.

Don found himself full of a sadistic sexual power as he began fucking his wife's back passage brutally, his own excitement growing as he felt her body reacting and her whimpering words spill out between screams. He used all his weight, and strength to drive his cock home and, as she screamed, he began sawing in and out in a wild, abandoned rhythm, determined to shoot his cum deep up into her anus and fill her adulterous, incestuous little belly to the bursting point.

Ned, his hips moving lewdly, his cock gliding in and out of Tina's mouth, watched his sister being savagely ass-fucked and felt his own brutal excitement growing. And, as he watched, he saw Kathy's body slowly begin to roll and writhe like a bitch in heat, saw her firm, rounded young breasts jiggle obscenely on the mattress below her. The expression on her face was changing from intense pain to intense pleasure. The sounds torn from her throat were turning to moans and mewls of pleasure. "Fuck! She's loving it!" he said in a whisper of disbelief.

And Kathy *was* loving it! She was beyond the pain now and loving her humiliation!

"F... f... fuck me harder, d-darling!" she breathed ecstatically.

"Don!" Ned called, "turn her over and we'll both give her cock!" his brother-in-law called.

In his savage lewd mood, Don found he was capable of doing anything. Ned's suggestion seemed like a way for him to show his further contempt. Holding Kathy tightly by her slim waist, his cock buried in her anus, he rolled her over on top of him until she lay sprawled, her breasts and legs spreading, her hairy cunt wetly gaping in all its pink, aroused glory.

Her brother and the other girl hurried to the bed and looked at her loveliness as she lay with her legs spread wide, the hilt of her husband's cock buried deep up in her wide-stretched asshole and her cunt wet, wide, and waiting. Instantly, her brother was on top of her and shoving his virile young cock deep in her open, dripping cunt while she moaned and tried to move in time between them. She

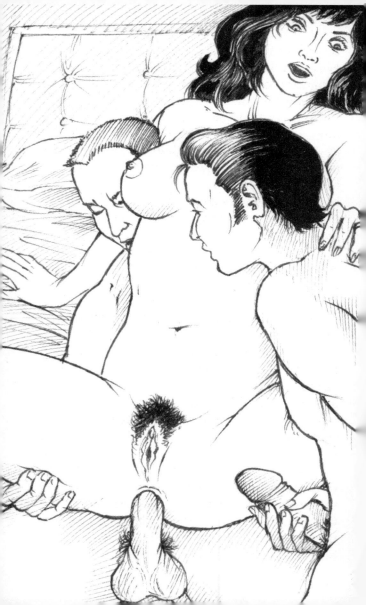

could feel the two hardened male cocks inside of her, moving independently of each other, separated only by a thin wall of excited flesh between rectum and vagina.

The Indian girl was on the bed, lying next to the trio. "Me next!" she breathed as she caressed their bodies and kissed their mouths. Each of them pawed and caressed her nakedly twisting body with their free hands as they began moving in rhythm to one another, building toward the wildest of orgasms ever.

"Do it to me," the tightly sandwiched Kathy cried through lust contorted lips, "fuck me... fuck me harder... I want to come... Please, oh, God, I want to come so bad..."

The dually fucking cocks, husband and brother, plunged into her again and again, grinding and twisting their hips lewdly as they fucked crazily in and out of her wide-stretched cunt and rectum. The two men could both feel their balls begin to swell and ache as the beautiful, naked young body of their wife and sister began suddenly to writhe even more violently between their sweating bodies.

Kathy whimpered again and again as the two cocks plunged deep up into her screaming belly, her husband's stretching the unexplored end of her rectum that gripped the sperm-swollen head like warm, buttery honey. Forgotten was the humiliation of being taken like a slut by her own brother and husband at the same time, or the obscene, pleading words still pouring half coherently out of her open mouth. All that mattered now was the wild, raging fire swirling out of control in her body flaming higher and higher by the two cocks fucking crazily into the dual passageways up between her widespread legs.

Kathy jerked her thighs back to open her cunt more to her younger brother as she felt his cock buried deep in her womb begin spurting hot and wet into her belly. At the same time, she ground her buttocks down tight onto the impaling cock of her husband as it, too, suddenly erupted deep up into her bowels. She squirmed tightly against both their groins, holding both the hotly spurting cocks deep in her body as her vagina and rectum both convulsed crazily sucking the last of her husband and brother's hot thick cream deep into bowels and belly. And then... she, too, screamed... as her own orgasm lashed like wildfire through her nakedly dancing body, the violence of her climax buffeting her helplessly between them like a rag doll. She writhed and twisted, clutching her younger brother tight in her arms and dropping her legs out to the side locked her feet tightly under the knees of her husband as she fucked out her passion like a wild, animal bitch in heat.

And then it was over. With a soft mewling sound her body went limp between them, her head rolling slowly to the side as a louder groan escaped her lips as the now half-hard cocks slipped wetly out of her sperm-flooded anus and vagina.

There was silence for a while, broken only by the heavy recuperative breathing coming from them all. And then, Kathy felt her legs being spread wide again and the softness of a girl's hair tickling her inner thighs as a greedily licking female tongue worked hungrily, purposefully, at the bruised lips of her open, sperm-filled pussy.

Oh, God, she thought to herself, is this what the camper and those teenage boys would have been like?

Chapter 8

The scene is upper New York state: a small, sleepy town of quiet respectability. Outside of town, there is a small junior college. The time is autumn – Indian summer – and the trees have burst in a riot of colour. Russets, reds, flaming oranges, and sun- bright yellows decorate the campus as leaves fall and whirl in the wind. There is the nipping hint of a cold winter to come in the air. Trent Gutenberg, the football coach waits on the commons for his friend, Johnny Bertolli, history professor, to join him. They will wend their way off campus to a local bar where they will have a drink and conversation before going home to their wives.

Trent sees Hank approaching, walking in his slouching way with his ever-present pipe dangling from his teeth. He looks beyond Hank, past his shoulder, as he sees Kathy Walters, Mrs. Don Walters, come out of the administration building and walk to the parking lot. Trent ran his fingers through his crewcut and nodded in her direction as Hank sauntered up. "Damn, don't know what it is, but I'd sure like to make it with that bitch." Hank turned to appreciate Kathy with sleepy eyes. As they watched, one of the students called, "Excuse me, Mrs. Walters, ma'am! May I have a word with you?" and ran to catch up with her.

"That?" Hank asked as they watched Kathy and the boy talking together. "Better forget about that. She's a real straight arrow. The word is out: she won't stand for any pass."

"Look at that figure," Trent enthused. "Damn, why does she dress like an old maid?"

"Like I said, she's pretty square and very much in love with a husband in Vietnam."

"Yeah. Too bad. There's just something about her, some kind of look on her face."

Hank laughed and slapped his friend on the back. "Forget it. Listen, of all the broads in this town that one is the least likely to come across. No hank-panky for Mrs. Kathy Walters, believe me."

Kathy's conversation with the young boy couldn't be heard. All the two instructors could see were their lips moving and their mouths smiling. An agreement was made and they said goodbye and Kathy went smiling to her car.

It might be hard to recognize her from the girl in Santa Monica of a few months before. She wore her hair in a tight severe bun. Horn rimmed glasses perched on her nose. She wore little or no makeup and her dresses were long and she generally wore tweed suits that helped to hide her voluptuous form. At the school, working in administration, she was known as cool and efficient, all business. The boys at the school seemed to like her and she seemed interested in their problems and could be seen talking with them on breaks and at lunchtime.

Tonight, she was driving home with a smile on her face. She rented a little house near the campus. She liked it because it was warm, friendly, and hidden from any neighbour's scrutiny.

At home, she read the day's mail. A curt letter from Don in Vietnam, saying the war was dragging on. A letter from Ned and Tina out in California, saying they were going to visit her next summer. She put the letters away and began preparing for the evening. Daylight saving made the dark come early and she smiled at the prospect.

Nightfall found her standing by the window, looking out, a drink and cigarette in her hand. It was a different girl from the one seen earlier on the campus. Her hair was let down to fall in wild billows. Makeup accentuated the sensuous features of her face. She was wearing high heels and black open-net stockings held in place by a garter belt. But no panties. A silk kimono slipped from one shoulder as she jiggled the ice in her highball and sipped as she looked down at the snowy mounds of her breasts naked under the kimono. The lights were low, music was playing on the tape recorder and soon, soon, those boys would be coming. Coming from the college, ostensibly on their way into town to see a movie. She closed her eyes and smiled. Young men with strong slim naked bodies and erect cocks, young boys so cruel and demanding in their youth, young men who would fuck her like a street whore and make her do obscene things. Young men who seemed inexhaustible and insatiable.

The doorbell rang and Kathy swallowed the rest of her drink before she went to answer it.

****

"What's your first name, Mrs. Walters, ma'am? Katherine, isn't it?"

The two youths stood awkwardly sipping their drinks, unsure of themselves, on the thick rug in front of the roaring log fire. Along with some strategically placed candles, it gave the room a warm, flickering light.

"That's right, Eddie. You can call me Kathy," said Kathy, smiling as she let the kimono slip entirely off her shoulders to reveal her superb breasts.

"That's a pretty name, and you sure are a pretty woman, Kathy," Eddie gasped. "And those titties sure are lovely, too," he said, his voice full of boyish bravado.

"Why thank you, Eddie. Would you and Richard like to touch them? The others are coming soon, but we may as well get friendly before they turn up, may we not?"

The two nineteen year-olds looked at her with something approaching adoration. And they devoured her breasts with hot, lingering glances. Kathy smiled and moved between her two young guests. Her hands slid under their blazers, down and down until they came to rest over each of the boys' crotches. She squeezed lightly until she could feel their cocks quickly hardening. Eddie's cock wasn't nearly as big as Richard's, she made a mental note. Well, he could go ass-side; she preferred a small cock in her ass. Richard, she decided, would have her cunt.

"Why – don't be shy, boys what are you waiting for? Aren't you going to get your clothes off? Or are you going to keep a lady waiting? Hmm?" and she moved her shoulders so that her lovely breasts jiggled and swayed provocatively. She had them just where she wanted them.

The boys tore their clothes off. She knelt between them, a hand on each of their quivering, naked cocks. Brazen, shameless, liberated, she thought, as she licked up the shaft of Richard's impressive pole.

"My, my, Richard, you have such a nice... penis!" Her voice rolled over the word like honey and cream, thick and rich, with a sort of suppressed quiver of lust in it. She took his cock into her mouth, her lips ovalling around it while all the while she worked at Eddie's, sliding the foreskin back and forth over the rosy glans. Sucking and licking them alternately, she brought the two young college boys to a pitch of moaning, gasping pleasure. She had them close to coming, and she loved that. She loved it for the excitement of the moment and for the knowledge that their youth would serve to get their cocks primed and loaded for another ejaculation. Perhaps more than just one. Besides, she knew the others would be here soon, most likely more than ready to take care of her own needs.

Richard came first, just as she moved her mouth off his cock to suck on Eddie's: the first burst hit her cheek, the next shot right over head and spattered in her hair; the third and fourth she caught on her tongue as she opened her lips to receive his creamy offering and the rest spurted over her bare breasts to drip down over her belly and adorn her thick pubic bush like pearls on black satin.

Then Eddie was gasping, shuddering and she turned to open her mouth and catch his cum-spewing cock, this time taking it deep into her mouth and relishing the spurts as they hit the back of her throat and she swallowed them down.

"Mrs. Walt... I mean, Kathy? Would you like me to, you know... eat you?"

Kathy smiled at the eager young buck.

"Why that's so sweet of you to offer, Richard. But there'll be plenty of time for that later on. So why don't you just relax and recover a little? Here, give me your glasses and I'll freshen them for you."   She went over to the bar and the two young males sprawled into the easy chairs either side of the fire listening to the music and lighting cigarettes, smoking, the flickering firelight playing on their lithe, muscular bodies. She fixed their drinks and her own then turned to join them.

She paused, smiling to herself and brushed her hair from her eyes as she took a big swig of the stiff drink that she had poured herself. She needed to be fortified for the coming evening. It promised to be a long one. For the next three hours. Five. Five young horny men alone with her.

There was a knock on the door, and she could hear voices outside. With a soft, throaty laugh, she shrugged on her kimono and went to open the door, murmuring to no one in particular, "Looks like I made it to that camper after all."

The End

Just a few of our many titles for sale...

The Young Governess
The first title in our Past Venus Historical imprint. Kate Spencer's job as governess to a young girl in a large country house seemed idealic. However, she is soon drawn into the Followers – a mysterious group who take pleasure in forcing young women to perform perverse sexual rituals.
£7.50

Satan's Virgin Twins
20-year-old twins Pam and Daphne and their friends must risk their bodies, their sanity and their very souls by taking part in obscene blasphemies and horrific sexual rites in order to thwart the Devil's grand plan to reclaim his earthly dominion. Set in the 1950s
£7.50

Orgy Girl
From the mansions of the Hamptons to the brownstones of Manhattan Karen Shaw is in demand as the Orgy Girl. In a spectacular, jet-setting round of outrageous sex parties and hedonistic fun with threesomes, foursomes and moresomes, Karen certainly proves herself to be no Barbara Cartland heroine.
£7.50

Salem's Daughters
The first title in our Past Venus Fantasy imprint. After centuries under the sod, warlock John Willard is more than ready to wreck vengeance on the decendants of the men and woman who sent him to the gallows, introducing them to incestuous perversions on a grand scale..
£7.50

Turkish Delight
After being cruelly raped by her callous husband on her honeymoon, Lucy Dean finds herself adrift in one of the most exciting and dangerous cities in the world: Istanbul. Drugged and abducted, she faces a life of sexual slavery, but first she must be taught the tricks of the trade.
£7.50